Caramel Kisses

TJ Michaels

Caramel Kisses ©
Copyright 2009-2015 by T.J. Michaels
Second Electronic Printing – 2015
First Paperback Printing - 2015
ISBN (13): 978-0-9905699-3-0
ISBN (10): 0-9905699-3-4
ALL RIGHTS RESERVED.

Chapter One

Sydni Cannes, Executive Vice President of International Shipping for Expedex, Inc., was in the damn clink.

Great. Just great. This was exactly what she got for trying to break out of her shell and get back into what most people called life and have some fun. Maybe even meet someone after her three year self-imposed relationship hiatus. And for her trouble she was in the local jail with sore feet, a jacked up hairdo and makeup that had to look like hell by now.

And it was all her sister's fault.

Charli had talked her into getting her groove on at one of the local clubs. From the depths of her overstuffed closet she'd pulled out a pair of fuck-me pumps, a skimpy leather skirt that showed off her toned legs and a modest but delicious snake print spaghetti strap tank top. Even in spite of the little jellyroll on her tummy, Sydni had felt downright sexy that evening. She'd danced and sweated—which was the fun part—and blown off corny pickup lines from men young enough to cause a scandal. While it had been utterly frustrating to learn her sister had picked a teeny bopper club, Charli had still

3

been right—it had temporarily taken Sydni's mind off both work and how long she'd been without a steady boyfriend.

But bad luck and even worse timing landed her here with a bunch of women that looked like they could take on Mike Tyson in a fist fight.

The only thing that had gone right was the fact that she'd gotten talked into clubbing on a Sunday night. Which meant she only had to spend one night in jail before going in front of the judge on Monday morning, grateful not to have to spend another day wearing the same funky clothes.

First order of business for the day was Sydni's case. Looking as rough as hand cut wood, she stood when the judge entered the courtroom.

"State your name."

"Sydni Cannes, Your Honor."

After all the preliminary blah, blah, blah type stuff he asked, "You understand why you're here, Miss Cannes?"

Actually, she had no idea, so she responded with an honest, "No, your honor."

Then the judge proceeded to give her a scathing set down for something she hadn't even done, all while acknowledging she indeed hadn't done anything. What the hell kind of sense did that make? The portly fellow wrapped himself in an extra layer of condescension as he described the luxuries and privileges to be had in jail — snarky bastard — and give advice on how a woman "her age" could avoid these kinds of situations. Riiight.

Boiling mad, and none too embarrassed, Sydni bit down hard on the inside of her cheek, fighting to keep a stranglehold on her emotions. Lord, if she opened her mouth something in the smart aleck department would escape and make the situation worse.

"Okay, let's get down to it." The judge's impatience crackled in the air. "The charges against you are…"

"Excuse me. Drew Caruth, attorney at law. I'll be representing Ms. Cannes. I apologize for being late, your honor. I was just made aware of Miss Cannes situation." The voice came from the back of the courtroom followed by the cadence of determined footsteps.

Aw, hell. She recognized that voice.

Sydni's head swung around. Her mouth dropped open the moment her gaze stuck itself to that of the most handsome man she'd ever seen walking around the Expedex offices these past few months. Though they worked for the same company, they didn't work in the same department. In fact, they were seldom on the same floor, thank god. All Sydni really knew about this man was the effect he had on the goofball females of the company. It seemed that any woman walking down the hall at the same time as him fell under some ridiculous spell. After he passed they fanned themselves, made little "mmm" sounds, and giggled like children.

Sydni pretty much kept her distance from just about all of the men like the plague, except those she worked closely with. After all, Expedex, Inc. was her career, not her family. She worked — and worked damn hard — for a company that held more than one-third of the market share in shipping international goods. But just because she kept herself buried in her duties didn't mean she was blind. The man was a god and a half.

Even as tired and distraught as she was, Sydni couldn't help but notice the trim, broad shouldered delight was all suited up in a dark gray double-breasted affair with a black shirt and classic striking tie. The suit matched a pair of sparkling eyes, gray as the sky during a spring rain, and shielded by long dark lashes a woman would die for. Midnight black, tastefully cut hair had a hint of wave in it, and his skin held a healthy glow, like he'd spent just the perfect amount of time in the sun. Whew, goodness! Too young for anything other than gobbling him up with her eyes, he no doubt ranked high up in the uber-scorching-hottie department.

Then Sydni's head tilted as a thought flew out of right field and hit her right in the temple — what the hell was Drew doing here on a Monday morning rather than at the office? But there was no time to dwell on it. Instead she blinked in awe when the unexpected lawyer spoke up and pretty much took it from there. She hoped he knew law as well as he dressed. If so, she'd be out of here in an hour.

And if not? No, she wouldn't think about that.

All she had to do was keep her awkwardness at being bailed out by a co-worker in check long enough to get the hell out of dodge. Wait a minute, if Drew knew she was here, yet the man was nowhere near that club where she'd been busted last night... Oh god. Somebody else had to have spilt the beans on her. Embarrassment morphed into mortified.

Her face heated to an alarming degree. Oh my god. Please, just get me out of here fast.

Erecting a façade of her typical cool demeanor, Sydni tuned back in to what was being said around her. She squashed all the questions swimming around in her mind when Drew turned and asked the judge if he could approach the bench.

Glad the table in front of her hid most of her practically bare legs, the fact slammed home that her life and reputation were in the hands of someone she didn't really know. But would she look a gift horse in the mouth. Not bloody likely.

Next thing she knew, it was over.

"You are free to go, Ms. Cannes. All charges have been dismissed and I don't want to see you in my courtroom for anything else. Not even a parking ticket."

The knots she hadn't even realized were lodged in the pit of her stomach suddenly loosened. Sydni held her breath to suppress the sound of relief trying to push itself up and out of her throat. Given her recent, er, adventure, surely the sound would have been something between a hilarious crow and a relieved yet semi-horrified snicker. Neither of which were wanted at the moment.

The one-size-fits-all jailhouse orange flip flops flapped noisily against the smooth tile as she, Drew and an accompanying officer headed toward the room where she would be processed and released.

"Wow," she sighed tiredly. "I'm beyond relieved this is over. Thank you, Drew....what's your last name again?"

The young lawyer who'd represented her case raised an arrogant brow, then grinned with an all-male "well, what did you expect?" expression. That grin made her want to smack him in the back of the neck.

"It's Caruth. Drew Caruth." And proceeded to look her up and down like she was today's special at the local diner. "I'm in the South American imports division, a couple floors up from your offices."

She scowled for all she was worth, annoyed that the skin on her arms tingled at his perusal. And how did he know where her office suite was in a twenty-six floor building, anyway? Instead of asking him what she really wanted to know, she simply said, "I'm sure I've seen you somewhere other than Expedex, right?"

Instead of an answer, the man smiled. And it was a full, all out smile. None of that one-sided smirk stuff. The second he showed his pearly whites, his eyes sparkled as he met and held Sydni's gaze. All thoughts of whacking him melted away. Drew was a damn charmer, a combination of gorgeous and cocky. Not a good mix and he was so not her type. But then again, he was awfully dreamy looking. What the hell? Her head certainly seemed to be doing plenty of flip flopping today.

Two steps away from the processor's counter, Sydni's common sense slammed back into place as a stern-faced female cop handed her a large plastic bag. Syndi turned away from the scowling reject from Helga's House of Pain and dug into the bag containing her personal effects. "Wait, I need to make a phone call. Aw, damn it," she snapped. Her cell was dead.

"Here" Drew offered, holding out a sleek little silver number. Sydni hesitated. "It's okay, Sydni. I'm a friend of your sister's. In fact, she's expecting your call right about now so why don't you use my phone?"

Friend of Charli's? What was that about? This was just too perfect and going way too smoothly. And when Drew spoke a single word into the mouthpiece of the phone and it automatically dialed Charli she knew something was up. Sydni knew she was less than polite but couldn't stop herself grumping as she snatched the phone from his fingers.

"Syd? Syd is that you?"

"Uh, yeah. Charli, what the hell is going on?"

"I guess you've met Drew. Didn't he tell you what happened?"

"Well, no. We haven't really had a chance to talk. I just signed myself out of damn jail. That's the last time I go anywhere with you, damn it."

"Get off the phone already. You can fuss at me when you get home. I'll meet you at your house."

"Wait, aren't you coming to get me?"

"Girlfriend, are you blind and crazy? Don't you see that fine-assed man who just got your ass out of jail? And not only is he good looking, but he'd be more than happy to give you a ride."

Turning away from Drew, she covered the mouth piece and hissed, "And just how the hell do you know that, young lady?"

Drew chuckled and she turned the evil eye on him. He threw his hands up in man's universal "I give" gesture and backed up a step. But the bastard was still grinning. Sigh. And what a devastating grin it was. She turned away with a barely suppressed growl.

"Never you mind," Charli replied. "Just get home. I'll fix you breakfast and fill you in."

"You sure as hell will. And you'd better not be matchmaking at a time like this." Sydni snapped the phone shut and handed it back to her newly acquainted lawyer. "Look, I don't know you so I'm trying to reserve judgment, but just what are you and Charli up to? I sure as hell don't remember her telling me she was dating a guy named Drew."

"That's because she isn't. Now about that ride?"

And it looked like that was all she was going to get out of him, other than a lift to her front door. Damn man.

They made quick work of finishing up her business and headed out the back to the parking lot.

Drew couldn't believe how things had worked out. Who would have thought that the woman he'd secretly ogled for what felt like a century would end up in such a predicament? While surely uncomfortable for her, it couldn't have been more perfect from where he sat. In fact, Charli had said as much when she'd called him at two o'clock in the morning begging him to bail her sister out of jail.

First off, he couldn't believe a woman as classy and untouchable as the Unsinkable Sydni Cannes would find herself behind bars. Second, he'd been asking Charli to introduce him to her again since the first time they'd met a year ago at a high-class shindig thrown in Charli's honor.

Hell, Sydni hadn't known he was alive then. And if not for her little stint with the law, she wouldn't know he was alive now. Even working in the same building for the same firm he hardly ever saw her in the company café, the parking lot or any place else he tried to make of habit of running into her at. In fact, he'd thought perhaps she deliberately avoided him. But that was absurd. This woman had her life together. She was fine as his favorite dessert wine, and on top of her game in her career. And if all she'd done for her sister was any indication, Sydni was an all out go-getter, yet genuine and giving. Just what he wanted in a woman, mind, body and soul.

When he'd walked into that courtroom and saw her standing there Drew had been brought up short for a second. Even after having spent the night in jail the woman set his pulse racing and his imagination skating to catch up with it. What a big difference from the stylish pants suits she typically sported. The woman had on the sexiest little black leather skirt tailored so perfectly it seemed like someone poured it over her hips. But the killer was, in spite of sporting a pair of cheap plastic-and-foam jailhouse flip flops, the things still managed to make her calves look sculpted and her legs go on forever. Dayum!

In the four months he'd been at Expedex, Drew had seen Sydni plenty of times, but always from a distance. In fact, she seemed to hold herself apart from everyone, not in a cold way, but… Drew couldn't quite put his finger on it. Even at Charli's party, Sydni had managed to stay somewhat detached from her guests, always keeping Charli the center of attention, introducing her to high dollar potential clients.

But this morning was different. No "across the room" interlude or long distance gazes. Today he'd been within a foot of Mizz Cannes. He'd expected the attraction he'd felt for her to dance around in his gut at being so close, but what he hadn't expected was the need to take care of and protect her. Nor had he foreseen the insane sexual craving that made the blood boil down through his arteries.

She'd been a picture of concern and vulnerability with a slight edge of "pissed off". Beautifully steaming mad. And god, he wanted her.

After the proceedings, Sydni grumbled the entire time she'd been in his car going home, but Drew didn't give a rat's rear end. Today, one of his prayers had been answered—he'd gotten a foot in the door with Sydni Cannes. And he was determined to get his whole body through then stick to her like glue.

* * * * *

Fresh out of a shower and the funk of the inhabitants of the county jail washed away from her skin, Sydni eased into the kitchen. Charli shooed her toward a high pub chair at the kitchen counter and Sydni moaned with delight. Her sister had created a decadent homemade breakfast of mascarpone-filled crepes with fresh strawberries and honey poured liberally on top.

"Mmm, this is so perfectly good it almost makes up for the blunder of the century. I'm so sleepy I don't know what to do. And before you ask, hell no, I did not get any sleep in jail. Too busy watching everybody else watching me." She licked a bit of strawberry juice from her spoon and laid it down on the breakfast tray just long enough to fuss. "That is the last time I go out with you, woman," Sydni grumbled around a mouthful of the best crepes she'd ever had.

"It's not my fault the heel broke off your shoe on the corner of the worst street in the Fillmore district," Charli defended. "Nobody in their right mind would associate you with those hookers on the corner. First, you're too classy by half, and second, when the police started rounding 'em up, you would think they'd have paid closer attention to who they were grabbing off the street."

"Well, it's your fault for talking me into going to that raunchy club in the first place. You could have at least warned me that some local celebrities were going to be at the place," Sydni said with no small amount of snark. "I would have avoided it like the plague. All those skanky women showing all their asses just hoping to get the attention of some celebrity-fied pimp."

"But Syd, it's not my…"

"Whoa, it is in fact all your fault. It is all your fault I broke my shoe trying to run to the car in the rain. It is all your fault you left me standing on the corner while you went to get the car. And it is definitely all your fault that the cops picked that exact moment to raid the 'ho stroll." Charli laughed like a loon regardless of Sydni's fierce scowl. "I don't care what the issue is, it's your fault, Charli. If it rains, your fault. My laptop dies, your fault. I gain ten pounds while taking a purge, your fault. Get it?"

"Okay! Fine." Charli cracked up. "But you can't deny you had a good time. Well, until you got arrested."

"Speaking of getting arrested, how did you pull off finding that lawyer on the fly? When he dropped me off, I was relieved he simply opened my car door for me, waved at you like your best girlfriend and got the hell out of here. God, how embarrassing to be saved by a co-worker. Hell, to be saved by anyone. Anyway, he seemed familiar as if I'd seen him somewhere other than the office, but I can't place him."

"We went to law school together. Have been good friends ever since. When I saw them carting you away, he was the first person I thought of to call. God, Syd, I completely forgot that he was working at your place now. He's only been there, what, a couple of months?"

Sydni shrugged. No point in worrying about it now. "Well, girlfriend, he's quite a catch," Sydni said around a swig of orange juice. "He said you two weren't going out, but if he's single, you should. You two would make a cute couple. You know, your cocoa to his vanilla? Go on, girl."

"We're not dating. Just friends. Besides, I'm not his type."

"What? Is he gay or something? Maybe you can convert him, girl."

"Drew? Gay? Not even close!" Then she laughed like a sailor who'd been told the raunchiest joke on the high seas. But then came that sideways look Charli flashed whenever she was up to something. Sydni nibbled on her bottom lip and eyed her sister closely. Hmm, what was that about?

"I swear I'm not up to anything!" Charli threw up her hands and blurted the words before Sydni could even ask, which meant she was most definitely up to something.

"You'd better not be. The last thing you want is my sore size nines planted up your backside."

"Yes, ma'am," Charli demurred with a big bright smile. "As for Drew, he graduated top of his class and passed the bar on the first go. You remember, he was at the grand opening party for my boutique."

"No, I don't remember. As for lawyer related topics, I still can't get over the fact you went to law school, passed the bar exam, then decided to become a fashion designer, er, tailor."

"Yeah, but I'm a highfalutin tailor," Charli sassed.

After clearing the dishes, a bit of sisterly hugging and laughing over Sydni's stint in the hooskow, and the thankfully dismissed charges, the two ladies kissed, made up and set plans to get together for a family dinner the following weekend.

Before driving away, Sydni's only sister planted another big wet smack on her cheek and said, "I'm glad everything worked out, Syd. You've taken care of me forever. You deserve to be happy. You're the best sister a girl could have and I love you."

Sydni held back the tears gathering behind her eyes at the tenderness pouring out of her sibling. She felt cherished, special…even if nobody loved her but Charli.

With a sigh, she watched Charli put her little black sports car in reverse and back out of the driveway.

Sydni thought about dragging herself up to bed. An image flashed into her brain of herself laying in the big king-sized number with her body wrapped around an oversized pillow. Going to bed lost its appeal, especially when one side of it was always empty and cold.

But Sydni was a realist. She'd been so devoted to taking care of Charli she'd already missed the "family and kids" boat. At her age, most women were settled into their families by now while all she had was work. Hell, her biological clock had stopped ticking so long ago she was sure the thing had suffered battery corrosion. And there was no expectation for a damn thing to change now.

Oh well, may as well get back to work. Sigh.

Chapter Two

A mousy male voice whispered into the darkness.

"Sydni Cannes suspects something."

After a moment of silence, Alex urged her lover to turn over and settle on his hands and knees. She licked a scorching path up his spine, peppering him with a combination of open mouthed kisses and blunt questions. He was quite delicious, if somewhat boring.

"How do you know?" A bite to the supple flesh of his left ass cheek elicited a gasp from the recipient of her sharp nips.

"S-she called me to her office and…oh god," the pawn gasped. The cock Alex boldly explored throbbed wildly beneath her fingers.

"Continue," she whispered sharply, tugging on his full sac.

"I went to her office. The invoices associated with the purchase order for the Sony shipping contract didn't…aahhh! Didn't add up. Please. Please…"

A wild sigh ensued, followed by thrashing hips that sought fulfillment of the need Alex carefully cultivated.

"Tell me the rest. Now." It came out a cold command. But not cold enough to douse the flames of the rock-hard rod in her hand.

"I-I told her that the rest of the invoices were probably waiting to be s-sent. That it could be as s-simple as an accounting technicality."

"Did she buy it?"

"Oh god, yes!" Pant. Gasp. "Yes, she bought it."

"Good boy." One hand petted the sensitive balls underneath the pawn's weeping penis, carefully slipping a single finger into the pawn's puckered hole. The other hand remained wrapped around his cock, pumping roughly. Down around the base, then up to sweep over the sensitive glans. Alex's mouth followed it, greedily taking him to the very back of her throat just as the finger in his ass tickled his prostate. The pawn spun into oblivion, the intensity of his orgasm expressed in a screech as he came so hard he didn't notice she'd neither kissed, nor swallowed.

Not five minutes after seeing the pawn to the elevator, Alexandra headed to the shower. She flipped the water on, adjusted it to the desired temperature. And brooded.

After all, Sydni Cannes wasn't a high six-figure Executive Vice President for nothing. The woman's division had closed more multi-million dollar deals than any other in the entire company, ever. She alone was responsible for getting goods manufactured in Japan into the hands of consumers a full six months before the competition. Sharp didn't begin to describe Cannes. And that was exactly what would get Alex's ass in a sling if she didn't find a way to advance her plans. Shit.

Sydni Cannes was a whiz at negotiating contracts. But negotiating wasn't the issue here. The Sony deal had been won, closed and was currently being expedited. So why was Cannes digging into this particular one? Usually once a deal was closed, only the project manager responsible for executing the details bothered to revisit the actual documents signed by all parties. Alex knew she had to move faster, or get caught with her hand in the cookie jar.

Her first thought was to discredit Cannes. But how? The woman was untouchable, her position in the company solid, and her reputation as spotless as newly fallen snow. Hell, last Alex heard, Cannes had been seen at the lake south of town, walking on water.

Sigh. Snatching her cell up off the tiled counter Alex hit the speed dial, leaned back against the wall and closed her eyes. Her stomach danced from one side of her belly to the other. Strange how she craved and dreaded talking to the man whose smooth sexy voice floated through the earpiece.

"What?" Viktor asked flatly.

"I have the info we need. Are you coming over?"

"Depends on whether it'll be worth my while."

"It'll definitely be worth your while in more ways than one. I promise." No answer. Not even a hint of interest. Time to up the stakes just a little bit. She knew the bastard liked to make her beg for it. Damn, and she loved groveling for him. "How 'bout a trade, lover? My info on Sydni Cannes…"

"In exchange for a good, hard fuck?"

Alex's breath caught in her throat for a sec as she let the raunchy words and heated — finally — tone of Viktor's words wash over her. "Oh yes. I think that'll do."

"In that case I'll see you in half an hour."

Her belly fluttered in anticipation of the pleasure promised by the hard-edged, deep, masculine voice. Mmm, hard, deep…exactly what she wanted.

"Use your key. I'll await you in bed," Alex purred, then snapped the phone shut. She jumped into the shower and washed up at record speed, paying special attention to freshly shaving her oh-so-ready pussy.

* * * * *

After a hard day at the office bled into an even harder evening at home, Sydni switched off her laptop and wrinkled her nose in confusion. The numbers for the new shipping contract she'd landed still didn't line up. Something was off but she was no closer to nailing it down right now than she'd been when she'd discovered the issue a couple of days ago.

Perched in the middle of a sea of cushions and covers all over her big comfy bed, the sexily dim lighting of the fireplace had her mind drifting elsewhere…mainly to a topic she'd been thinking too much of lately — sex. And lots of it.

It had been a whole week since her little run-in with the law yet any thought of that event instantly conjured the ruggedly handsome Mr. Drew Caruth. Sydni just couldn't stop thinking about him. In fact her fantasies of late featured sun laden black sand beaches, hunky real-life lawyers and all kinds of naughty possibilities that sent her temperature soaring.

She jumped when the phone rang.

"Hello?" she grumped, hopping out of her personal haven of silken sheets and ran down to the kitchen.

"Is this Ms. Sydni Cannes?"

"Yes, who is this?"

"This is Earl Matheson from KWQQ, your radio station for smooth jazz."

"Uh, okay. How can I help you, Earl?"

Tilting the handset so she could hold it on her shoulder and still snatch the Häagen-Dazs Butter Pecan ice cream out of the freezer. Grabbing a spoon, she headed back upstairs. Treating herself for landing the big Sony account was overdue. She deserved this damn ice cream, and no one was going to interrupt her long overdue indulgence. Not to mention Earl was spoiling a perfectly good evening of masturbating in between TV shows.

"It's not what you can do for me, but what we want to do for you."

"Okay, Earl, I'm not trying to be rude but I'm in the middle of something." Yeah, in the middle of creaming your fingers. "You've got thirty seconds to get to the point then I'm going to have to go. Deal?"

"Deal. Let's cut to it. Your sister, Charli, has entered you in our Set 'Em Up, Knock 'Em Down contest."

"I'm sorry, Earl. I don't bowl."

The man laughed, really laughed. Hard. Like she was the biggest idiot in all of creation.

"Okay, Earl, you're down to about ten seconds here, bud."

"Your sister has basically set you up on a blind date. You are to meet your mystery man at a place of your choosing tomorrow morning at exactly eleven o'clock. And since your sister knows the person it's perfectly safe."

"Two seconds."

"No problem, Sydni. Let us take down your information on where you want to meet this dream date and we'll take care of the rest. You can even choose what he has to wear so you'll recognize him. You two hit it off, we'll send you to a five-star dining establishment and tell your story on the air. If not, we'll pay you for your time."

"And this was my sister's idea?"

"Yep. Miss Charli Cannes wrote to us when she heard about the contest and her letter as to why you should get the dream date was picked unanimously by our staff. Would you like to hear the letter? We can even get her on the phone if you like."

"No. I believe you." *Damn woman. Just wait, I'm gonna strangle her, then resurrect her just so I can kill her again.*

"What was that, Ms. Cannes?"

"Uh. Nothing."

"So will you do it?"

"Yes. Okay. What do you need?"

Fine. Anything to get the man off the phone. She'd deal with Charli later. Meddling girl.

After a few minutes spouting off the most outrageous clothing she could think of for her so-called dream date to wear, Sydni hung up the phone and scooted down in the covers.

The ice cream carton settled onto the nightstand with a soft thunk. The spoon clattered against the wood just before Sydni's eyes slid closed. Her tongue was cool against her lips as it slid from one side of her mouth to the other while her mind conjured the delicious image of…Drew? Again? What the hell?

Why was she thinking about that Drew guy so much? She shouldn't be filling her mind with pictures of the one man every single female in their whole company wished would push them up against the nearest solid object and fuck them into oblivion. God, the man couldn't be more than thirty years old. But damn he was a fine specimen of a man. Hell, a simple look her way made her knees knock together. But Drew wasn't interested in her. Why would he be when there were plenty of other women his age that made it more than clear that they were interested?

The man could get any piece of tail he wanted. And learning he was a good friend of Charli's just added to the list of why he was off limits. Too young. Too damn fine. Sigh. Just the thought of his hands on her made her go red in the face. No, she shouldn't…but then again, who'd know?

The second the thought formed in her head, a pair of gray eyes appeared behind her lids. Drew. A sexy smile lit up his face just for her. And in her fantasy, that face moved closer and closer to her own until he was close enough to kiss, but not quite. Instead, he dipped his head and nudged her chin up so he could inhale the fragrance of her skin. With nothing touching her but the tip of his nose, Drew explored the soft underside of her jaw before nuzzling his way toward the hollow behind her left earlobe.

Talented fingers touched her intimately, gently twisting a nipple before drawing it into his mouth, pulling deeply. Sucking hard, then laving the tip, round and round.

Breathing deeply, Sydni imagined Drew's scent filling her nostrils. His tongue slid down the side of her neck and left a warm, wet path down to her collar bone. Her hips swiveled in a slow, deliberate circle as one hand closed around a swelling breast and the other slid between dewy labia. She wasn't even surprised at how wet she was—it was becoming the norm with thoughts of Mr. Caruth, damn it.

And now her clit needed some attention. Reaching into her nightstand drawer, her favorite toy fell comfortably into her hand. Anxious and ready for relief, Sydni ignored the feeling of emptiness in her womb. Spreading her slick and swollen flesh she aimed for her clit and flicked the switch.

"Aw, damn it," Sydni grumped at herself. The batteries were dead.

A quiet gasp and a sexy masculine moan snapped her attention to the TV she'd forgotten was on. Her favorite vampire was laying some hot, hard, sweaty sex down on a female like he'd never have another chance. Afterward, he loved her so tenderly it brought tears to Sydni's eyes even as her fingers slid over the planes of her tummy.

"Obviously this date couldn't have come at a better time. Look at you, alone on a Friday night blubbering over a television show. You need to get laid, woman. Seriously."

Maybe the date with Mr. Unknown tomorrow morning would lead to a little bump and grind? Sydni snorted at herself, knowing she had every intention of meeting the man just long enough to blow him off.

Chapter Three

She must be nuts. What the hell was she doing here waiting for a total stranger? Sydni hated to admit she'd been so engrossed in her work, she'd completely forgotten about the weird phone call from the DJ at KWQQ until one of their admins had called with a reminder of her "appointment with destiny". God, could you get any more corny? And when the radio chick rattled off what her mystery man would be wearing, at her request of course, all Sydni could do was shake her head knowing she'd been cruel.

She checked her watch with a huff and felt the muscles in her stomach tighten. It was almost time. And though she wanted to have an attitude about the whole set up, Sydni couldn't manage to get mad at her sister. Sure, Charli had signed her up for the stupid radio station's blind-date contest, but the woman hadn't tied her hands and feet to make her come here to meet the man. Well too late now. If there was one thing she wouldn't do, it was stand someone up. It was simply too rude. But she could get rid of the guy tactfully. And quickly.

So here she sat at a stupid Starbucks instead of sleeping in, waiting for a man dressed in one of those stretchy workout shirts done in ghastly neon green, and a pair of black and white checkered golf pants. She shuddered at the ghastly image in her mind. Well, one thing was certain—any man with enough balls to walk into a busy Starbucks at a major intersection dressed like that must be as hard-up as she was.

Sydni laughed at herself, then ratcheted back to a semi-hilarious giggle when two women at the table next to hers flashed sharp looks. She should have been embarrassed to burst out laughing in the middle of a coffee shop while she sat alone, but after the week she was having, who gave a good goddamn? The only thing on her mind was getting this over with so she could go home, curl up on the couch with her favorite faux fur blankie and get some work done. Perhaps while listening to a rerun of the season opener of her favorite vampire soap opera.

"And pretend not to be lonely. Damn it." Oops. She hadn't meant to say that out loud.

Syndi snuck a peek at the two ladies who'd given her the stink eye seconds before. They were no longer eyeing her. Their attention was on someone across the room. When one of the ladies mouths edged open as if she were on the verge of drooling, Sydni had to see what the hell she was looking at. Was there a life sized piece of sculpted chocolate on display or something?

Sydni turned to look and her own lips eased apart. Oh god, this was so not happening.

There across the room, walking confidently in her direction was a man. Correction, a freakin' hot studly construction worker mountain-type man…in a neon green stretchy workout shirt, hideous checkered golf pants. And a familiar face.

Sydni looked up at the ceiling and prayed. "God, just come and take me now, please. No? Well, how 'bout opening the floor up and letting me drop through it? No on that one too? Damn."

"Hi Syd."

She was going to wake up anytime now, right? Right, damn it!

Then he spoke again. Sigh. Guess her prayers weren't working today.

"I said, hello Syd."

"Uh, hi, and it's Sydni. Sid-nee. Fancy seeing you here, Mr. Caruth."

"It's Drew, and yep, definitely fancy."

Now what were the odds that her recently

acquainted lawyer would be the guy the radio station—correction, Charli, damn it—had set her up with? Why the hell hadn't she figured it out sooner? Duh! And who would have thought the designer suits he wore in court hid such a fantabulous physique? Sydni'd thought he was only broad shouldered, but boy had she missed the mark by at least a football field.

The ugly shirt he wore left very little to the imagination, for goodness sake. Short sleeved, it showed off perfectly tanned, ropey muscled forearms and biceps sparingly dusted with black down. The shirt was stretched so tightly across his chest every can in the six pack was visible and his pecs were deliberately formed mounds of muscle. The whole lot tapered down to a trim waist and…

Nope. No way. I will not look down any further.

Okay, that declaration lasted all of half a second.

And down her gaze strayed right to a…hey, what was up with that? No overly impressive bulge? No huge package? Maybe he'd shrunk up his dick from lifting all those weights? Gazing a bit lower, disappointment was certainly wiped out of her mind at the man's legs. His trousers fit perfectly, not too tight in the hips and thighs, but were cinched in at the waist. Since her sister was a lawyer-turned-tailor, Sydni could tell a living-room-alteration job on a pair of off-the-shelf pants at first glance. But Drew's black hideous checkered duds looked tailored, as if the only way to get a good fit was if he bought a size or two larger just to get his thighs into them, then have the waist adjusted. Athletes whose sports required a lot of leg strength usually had this issue because they're thighs were so large. And Drew looked like he fit that bill to the tee.

Amazing. Mr. GQ Lawyer stood there looking as deliciously sinful as her mama's rum poundcake. And he'd seen her rougher than rough after a night locked in the hooskow? Oh god, how embarrassing.

Sheer horror snaked through each limb and it must have made its way to her face.

"What's wrong. You look like you've just seen Hannibal Lecter."

"Uh, what? Oh sorry. Nothing. I was just thinking about what I must have looked to you the other day."

"You mean when we walked out of the courtroom?"

"Yep. That's the time. Look, coming here

was a mistake. I must have been out of my mind meeting a total stranger here."

"Not a total stranger, Sydni."

"Well, still. Why don't we just call it a day? Besides, I don't date guys I work with."

"But we don't actually work together, do we, beautiful?"

Beautiful? When was the last time she'd been called beautiful by someone who appeared to mean it? Sigh. That so wasn't the point.

She rose and stuck out her hand wondering if she really wanted him to shake it or not. Surely if he touched her she'd fall on the floor in a dead faint from lack of oxygen because lord knew she'd stopped breathing the second the images of what she'd imagined him doing to her flashed in her head.

He wrapped warm fingers around hers and eased her toward him. Leaning close, he whispered for her ears only, thank god.

"Well, I did a pretty good job getting your charges dropped, not to mention I wore this ugly ass outfit just for you. At least have lunch with me?"

His words ended on a friendly chuckle, but Sydni hadn't missed the confidence—and determination?—in them.

Arrogant bastard. Damn gorgeous, tall and yummily put together arrogant bastard. And he had a point, damn it. "So, how'd you get my charges dropped? I didn't know you did criminal law." Hell, she hadn't actually meant to ask him that, especially not out loud. The last thing she needed was for the man to start gloating or for the folks at the next table to think she was some kind of two-bit crack ho' with a neon green-shirted pimp.

"Actually, my specialty is contract law."

"What?! What were you doing negotiating my release? What if things had gotten screwed up?"

"It was a simple misdemeanor, Sydni. Any lawyer worth his salt could have gotten you off, even if his area of expertise was salt mining treaties. It was obvious you were simply in the wrong place at the wrong time. Besides, Charli wouldn't have trusted me with your situation if I didn't know what I was doing. She and I both trained in law, remember?"

"Yes, but…?"

"Well, it worked didn't it?" he said, tilting his head to the side in mock challenge.

She couldn't argue with that. The man was too attractive and too charismatic by half. And when he smiled the thought of proving her point flew right out of Sydni's head, replaced with the urge to kiss him. Repeatedly. Uninvited, her erotic fantasy in which he'd starred the night before mixed with the fact he'd sprung her from the big house. Immediately her cheeks up in flames. Thank god for dark skin.

"I'm gonna kill Charli," she muttered to herself.

"It was her fault I was there to get you out of the clink that morning, so don't be too hard on her, eh?"

Great. Now he had two points. Relenting, Sydni sighed, "Fine, what'll it be?"

They walked over to the counter together where Syndi ordered a simple Earl Gray tea, then motioned for him to place his order.

He cut the coffee maker babe a fleeting glance then turned a riveting stare on Sydni. The man's voice dripped with so much sensuality, Sydni wondered if she could find a way to put it in a patch, women the world over could simply slap one between their legs when they needed a fix. She'd make a fortune.

"I'll have the special dark roast." Then with a saucy little tilt of his head, eyes never leaving hers. "With a shot of hot caramel and a bit of creaming…uh, I mean cream stirred in." Then he winked.

Holy shit! Was he flirting with her? Pwah. Creaming indeed.

"Oh and I'd like the half-and-half steamed. Make it good…and hot."

One side — oh god, she really shouldn't be looking — of his perfectly formed mouth tipped up into a grin and the belly jiggle harpies came out to play. Definitely harpies 'cause her stomach was dancing to a tune much too hard and lively to be butterflies.

Sydni's tea came up first. They stood waiting for his drink as she sipped the steaming hot brew trying to get her eyeballs to behave. They wanted to roam all over the man, take him in from head to toe. She'd already let her gaze stray once and now the damn things wanted to take that particular journey over and over.

Back at their table, Sydni felt suddenly shy. It was such an unfamiliar emotion she lowered her eyes and kept her gaze plastered to the steam rising from her cup while she tried to figure out what to do with herself.

Drew chose that moment to lean in close. The natural scent of clean, healthy man wafted her way, sending a beacon blush to her cheeks.

Mentally screaming at her belly to stop flip-flopping, Sydni squeezed her warming thighs together and sipped the scalding hot tea. God, she wished an icy gale-force wind would blow through the building to cool her off. This was so not good. And for the life of her, Sydni couldn't think of a single reason why.

"You look awfully good today, Sydni," Drew crooned. He probably hadn't meant for it to sound so sexy, but oh well.

"I'm wearing a black sweat suit, Drew," she huffed, determined to resist the man's charm.

"Yes, but it's what's in the suit that makes it look so good. Now where should we go for lunch? As much as I love looking at you, I'm looking forward to eating. I'm so hungry I could just...feast." That last was said with more than a little innuendo. While it should have grated on Sydni's nerves, it strummed them instead.

It soon became urgent to change the subject because the current topic was heating up just a bit too quickly. And her goofy ass wanted to do the seventies disco shuffle while singing "Burn, Baby, Burn"!

With a brisk walk across the street to a little Italian deli, lunch was on. Once Sydni had been coaxed out of her shell a bit, the conversation flowed freely. They covered every subject from A to Z and soon a half-hour date turned into two hours. Sydni's general knowledge of, well, everything, combined with a wicked sense of humor had Drew laughing so hard he practically choked on his food more than once.

As their meal progressed, he found himself wanting to prolong their time together by any means necessary. Shaking his head at himself, Drew squashed down all the baser emotions the woman brought out of him. One moment he wanted to pamper her, the next he wanted nothing more than to touch her from her scalp clear down to her knees. He could see himself enjoying everything with her—a dumb B-movie, hot sweaty sex, a walk in the park, hot sweaty sex, or sitting in silence reading a book together, followed by...hot sweaty sex. Jesus, she'd turned him into a teenager eager to get his first taste of pussy!

A waiter cleared their dishes and dropped off a couple of slices of creamy cheesecake and a carafe of coffee. Drew poured Sydni a steaming cup. She eyed him like a snake in the grass, as if he'd bite when she least expected it. It was the same look she pinned him with when he'd opened the restaurant door for her, and again when he pulled out her chair. So he smiled and said, "Yes, I pour coffee, pull out chairs and open doors."

She tilted her head, but didn't say anything.

"I like to pamper the woman I'm with." Sliding the small container of cream her way, Drew watched Sydni stir her coffee while she watched him right back. She'd been having such a good time too. Almost seemed to be comfortable with him. Yet, something as simple as pouring her coffee put her right back on guard? What the hell kind of idiots had Sydni Cannes been out with where being nice put her back up?

Time to change the subject.

"Do you like board games, Sydni? Or any kind of games at all?"

"Believe it or not, I'm awesome at chess. As for other games, hmm…?" She tapped her chin, eyes focused upward while she thought. God, he could practically hear the gears grinding as she seriously considered the subject. In the seconds that followed Drew set a new target for himself – see to it that Sydni had more fun. If she had to think this hard about the kind of things she enjoyed, she obviously didn't do them enough.

Finally she said, "Well, I like movie trivia."

"Really? So do I. And since I have a thing for movies and beautiful black women…" With a deliberate pause, Drew let his gaze travel over her lovely features, then continued. "Let's try this on for size." Drew almost spewed his coffee at the utter shock that sent her chin toward the table as her mouth fell open. Okay, she needed more fun and more brash, blunt, straight up flirting. No problem. "You ready?"

She nodded with a still somewhat dazed expression. So he pushed on.

"Eartha Kitt." The tilt of Sydni's mouth and the glimmer of approval in her eyes said that she knew exactly who he was talking about. Eartha Kitt was still well known for her Catwoman purr, her flawless cinnamon skin and saucy attitude. "I don't think there's any early film star as sexy as Eartha Kitt. That woman used to give Batman a run for his money."

Drew took a bite of cheesecake. It was thick, creamy, delicious. He wondered if Sydni would taste just as sweet on his tongue. Her smooth flawless skin certainly reminded him of coffee and cream. Or maybe chocolate mousse ice cream. With Hershey nipples, er, Hershey Kisses. It was just enough to send a rush of blood streaking south until he had to fight the urge to adjust himself underneath the table.

"Did you know that Eartha Kitt played Catwoman in the Batman TV series between 1966 and 1968, but Lee Meriweather played the character in the movie of 1966?" he asked.

"Not even," Sydni retorted with a dismissive wave of her fork. "Everyone knows Eartha Kitt was the Catwoman of the 1960s. And that includes the movie. Nobody could purr like her."

"Wanna bet on it?"

The woman snorted, then chuckled. "I don't do bets, Drew."

Sydni might not do bets, but god he sure wanted to do her. The more time in her presence the hornier he got. And it wasn't just sex appeal. Sydni got to him on every level.

"I happen to be a total movie trivia expert, so I'll even go easy on you," he said smoothly, unable to hide what he knew was a shit-eating grin spread across his lips. The reaction was immediate. Just what he wanted. Well, almost.

All humor faded for a second before she snapped her well-known cool façade into place. He'd wanted to prick her pride, bring out her competitive edge, not piss her off. Time to tread a bit more carefully…then again, to hell with tip toeing around. Drew wanted Sydni to see him, the real him. Not the pretty playboy toy most women thought he was.

One perfectly manicured black brow winged upward as Sydni's neck canted to the left. "Make it easy for me? I don't need you to make anything easy on me, Drew. I've never done easy in my life. Besides, I'm not some simpering twenty year old just beginning to make her way in the world. I know who I am. And who I'm not," Sydni snapped quietly, stabbing her cheesecake like she was mad at it.

Ah, so that's her problem, Drew thought. Fine. He had no problem jumping right into what was really on the woman's mind. "What do simpering twenty year olds have to do with a bet over something fun and meaningless, like movie trivia?" Drew kept right on smiling. After all, even if she was mad, he was still enjoying her company. A soft huff and a couple of soft grumbles that sounded something like "damn man" and "off guard" told him she felt a bit on the silly side. But Drew also knew that the devil would be having blizzard weather before she admitted such a thing. Instead, she forced the frown from her brow and painted on an easy smile.

Meeting his eyes, she said, "Fine. Sorry 'bout that. What do you want to bet?"

"I bet you that Lee Meriweather was Catwoman in the 1966 Batman movie."

It sounded easy enough, but Drew knew his movies. Especially ones with sexy black women in them who pioneered the way for the current generations. Women like Eartha Kitt and Lola Falana. And it was a common misconception about who played what during those ground-breaking times.

"And what are you willing to wager since you're going to lose?" Sydni asked, all shameless confidence, showing almost every tooth in her mouth. She was all glowing confidence and feminine grace as she tilted her head again. But this time her almond shaped eyes twinkled with an expression as old as Eve. Drew laughed outright, ridiculously thrilled that she was flirting back.

Suddenly, Sydni went still.

Drew's laugh cut off abruptly when his eyes tracked Sydni's line of sight. He almost groaned aloud. His guffaw had caught the attention of the woman working the counter. The chick proceeded to tilt her head at a saucy angle and wink his way. What was it that urged these airheaded women to flirt shamelessly with a man, even when said man had another woman at his table? Not to mention the fact Drew wasn't paying anyone but Sydni the least bit of attention.

Totally ignoring the counter floozy, Drew said, "Since I'm determined to see you again, when I win I get a date and a kiss, not necessarily in that order."

"And if I win?" she asked. With eyes suddenly gone shy, Sydni looked down at the fork she was playing with. The tip of her tongue left a moist trail over her bottom lip. Drew wanted to taste her more than, than…hell, he couldn't think of a comparison just now. She made him feel untamed, wild. A lion. A predator. So high on his own testosterone he wanted to lift her onto the table and mercilessly tease her lush body until she spread her legs and yelled, "Do me now!"

"Well?" she asked.

Hell, he'd almost forgotten the question. Slowly reaching across the table, Drew took her hand in his and gently kissed the knuckles from left to right.

"I'll wear this ugly ass neon green workout

shirt for you again."

Now it was Sydni's turn to laugh outright as she took her hand back.

"You're on, handsome."

Handsome. Mmm. The word sounded so different, more meaningful, coming from Sydni. She probably hadn't meant anything by it. But in time, she sure as hell would.

They shook on the bet over the table.

Sydni was giddy as a sixteen year old on her first date until Drew pulled out his PDA, connected to the wireless internet connection offered by the restaurant and scooted closer to her in the booth. After a few clicks, a trip to the Wiki page for Batman 1966 proved her...wrong!

All she could do was gape at the traitorous PDA. And squeeze her thighs together when Drew chuckled sexily, promising all kinds of unspoken naughtiness. And right there in front of anyone who cared to watch, Drew more than made good on his word.

"Lunch tomorrow, Sydni. But I'll have that kiss now."

He scooted over to her side of the table and laid a kiss on her that started out so gentle it took her by surprise, lulling her into a sense of ease. Then he subtly upped the ante and drew her in with practiced skill. Sydni didn't realize the lip lock had already blazed out of control until she was moaning into his mouth, arms twined about his neck and holding on for dear life.

And when he walked her to her car he kissed her again. Sydni wasn't sure what surprised her more, the fact that he'd kissed her again, or that she hadn't pushed him away.

"What was that kiss for? Not part of the bet," she panted.

"That one was for good measure." With that he tucked her in, closed her door and walked away. *Dayum!*

Chapter Four

"Sooo," Charli drawled, "how'd your date go?"

"First, I've been meaning to tell you off since that radio station guy called me to set this whole thing up. Second, I can't believe you set me up with the same man who came to my rescue down at the county detention center knowing I'd have to see him at work. And third, I can't believe myself for agreeing to have lunch with him again tomorrow."

"Why lunch rather than dinner?"

"Charli, have you taken a good look at Drew? Being alone with him at night under any level of darkness, including moonlight, lamplight or other would be too much temptation."

"Something had to happen for you to say that, Syd," Charli giggled.

"Nothing happened." Oh lord, she was stammering. No wonder Charli snorted at her answer. Obviously her innocent act was totally not working.

With an impatient huff, Charli prodded,

"Syd, I've seen you blow off the smoothest pick-up lines from equally handsome men. For you to be this, this…itchy about Drew, something had to go down."

"I am not itchy."

"Uh-huh. Tell it to somebody else. Now spill it, woman," Charli challenged with a grin.

"Well, we had a little movie trivia bet and he won. The prize was a kiss. And boy did we, right there in the café. And after walking me to my car he, uh, kissed me again."

"Okaaay? Not like you haven't been kissed before."

"Yeah, but Charli, that kiss was…hell, I don't know how to describe it. Nobody's ever kissed me so…" She faltered, struggling to find words to express the connection she'd felt, the instant heat. The energy that spiked clear through to the ends of her hair. It was absolutely crazy to be this tooty over a man, any man, let alone one so much younger…and white on top of that, though she hadn't given it a second thought until just now. Good gracious, she was a mixed up something-or-other.

Regardless, there was no lying to Charli. "I mean, it was like I knew, simply knew, we'd be good together. And the man can kiss, I mean, not too much lip, not too much tongue, not too much touching, but just enough to set my damn skin on fire. Girl, I felt like a five-foot-four-inch melting chocolate woman. Too bad."

Charli laughed. Sydni could hear her sister clapping hilariously. Until she'd slipped in the "too bad" bit.

"Whoa, wait. What do you mean, too bad?"

"Girl, there's no way Drew and I can be together. But I have to admit the boy's got too much charm for his own good, and damn if I'm seriously unimmune to it."

"Boy?"

"Charli, he's what, thirty maybe?"

"A bit older than that, but so what? You're only forty-two, Syd."

"Are you kidding me? Girlfriend, I'm so not the rob-the-cradle type. We can leave that to my ex."

"Syd, are you still tripping over that? Just because your ex-boyfriend was a dog doesn't mean you'll be painted with the same brush simply because Drew is younger than you. Besides, you don't look a day over thirty-two yourself. And, if you're not interested in Drew, then why are you going to lunch with him again? He really digs you Charli. Has for a long time."

"It's just lunch, Charli, not marriage."

"Don't lead him on, Sydni." Charli's tone went hard, the words serious. Sydni's brows rose. She couldn't recall her sister ever speaking to her so protectively. What Charli was this on the other end of the phone line?

"Lead him on? Girlfriend, please. It's been so long since I've been in the game I don't even know how to do that to a man. Besides, I'm actually just looking forward to enjoying conversation with someone other than you," she chuckled.

"Aw, forget you," Charli quipped, sounding like her old self again.

"Besides, Charli, I'm sure he'd prefer to be serious with someone his own age."

"Huh? Why? What's someone his own age have that you don't have? You're damn fine, you take good care of yourself when you're not working yourself to the bone, and..."

Yeah, and her ass was spreading more every week in testament to how much time she spent at the office instead of walking or at the gym. Sydni almost turned to look behind herself and see how much further south her butt cheeks were than the rest of her body. Maybe Charli was right. Maybe she did work too much?

"Syd are you listening to me?"

"Huh? What?"

"Damn it, woman, you tuned me out. Fine, I'll just have to repeat myself. I said you need to spend time enjoying your life. You've got a great career with the corner office and a floor full of people who report directly to you. Not to mention a huge mini-mansion in which nobody totters around but you."

"I do not totter!"

"Oh sure, miss the point, why dontcha!"

"Point taken, Charli." Sydni felt her cheeks heat. They'd covered this subject way too many times in the past few years and she hated how right Charli was. Hated to admit that she was indeed beginning to feel lonely. But she wouldn't admit it to God himself. She cut across Charli's fussing. "Look, Charli, I know you care about me, but my choice in men has not been stellar. I don't plan on jumping into anything with anyone, including Drew. It's just a meal in broad daylight. And I meant it when I said I doubt he'd be serious about me anyway, so we'd have something in common."

"How can you say that about a man you don't know?"

Silence.

"You're right. That's really not fair is it?"

"Damn straight, Sydni. If you taught me anything, big sis, it's to give people a chance until they give you a reason not to."

Obviously she'd taught her sister well. And now it was coming back to bite her in the ass. But Sydni couldn't complain. Charli had indeed turned out to be quite a level headed young lady.

"Just enjoy the attention, Syd. You never know where it might lead. Could turn out to be the ride of your life."

Ride? As in hot, sweaty pounding-between-her-legs, ride? No, no, no. She shouldn't be thinking like that. She had work to do. Drew was simply a welcome distraction for lunch in between meetings. Nothing more, right?

Yeah, right.

* * * * *

The purchase order on Sydni's desk still didn't reconcile with the invoices charged against it. The number of shipments from Japan for that particular customer was well above the amount shown in the accounting documents, yet she was sure payments had already come in to cover the agreements. It was like the money had sunk into a black hole.

The intercom buzzed.

Sydni answered in perfect Japanese, "This is Sydni."

"Mr. Drew Caruth from S.A. division is here to see you, ma'am."

"Thank you, Tsubaki-san. Send him in."

Sydni ruthlessly squashed down the instant pounding of her heart. Looking at the man did funny things to her stomach so she kept her gaze plastered to the pages in front of her. Grrrr. It was so frustrating not to be able to spot the anomaly in the figures dancing across the page. Oh wait. The numbers weren't dancing, her eyes were crossing from staring at the damn things for so long.

She knew the second he entered. Not because she expected him, but because his presence filled the large space, seemed to reach for her. He moved closer and his subtle scent floated across the short distance between them, wafting toward her like welcoming fingers of a lover's hand.

"What's wrong?" Drew's voice floated to her from a few feet away.

"Hmm?" she asked distractedly.

"Your forehead is all scrunched up."

"Scrunched up?" Not the type of thing a lady liked to hear, damn it.

"Yes, scrunched, like you're thinking extraordinarily hard about something."

"It's nothing. Just work stuff."

"Looks like a contract," he said matter-of-factly.

"Uh huh..."

There was that niggling in the back of her mind again. And the longer she sat there, the more she knew what she needed to do. God, Sydni had hoped it wouldn't come to this, but it looked like she was going to have to get personally involved with this account. And that meant dealing directly with The Bitch—Alex Voltier.

Shit.

Drew's smooth, heat-inducing voice cut through her thoughts.

"Sydni, contracts are my specialty, remember? Want me to take a look at it?"

She regarded him for a moment, then decided she'd rather be somewhere relaxing with him instead of talking about work stuff. Now that was a first in a long time.

"Skip it. Let's get out of here."

"You sure?"

"Absolutely."

On the way out, Sydni stopped and gave her personal assistant a warm smile. "Tsubaki-san, I'm going to lunch. While I'm out please schedule a meeting between me and Alexandra Voltier." A meeting Sydni didn't look forward to. Alex was the project manager for the Sony small electronics contract. Dealing with the woman always felt as if she were setting herself up to be shot in the ass…or bitten by a snake. A venomous, slimy one.

* * * * *

Alex rose and closed the door to her office with a quiet snap. The picturesque view of the distant soaring mountains set against a backdrop of a jewel blue sky did nothing to improve her mood as she paced. With a deep breath, she turned away from the window and plopped down in her chair with a huff. Out of habit, the top of her pen was set in motion by her thumb with a click-click-click cadence.

Sigh. Nothing to be done for it. She had to call Viktor. Alex tapped her wireless earpiece, spoke into the voice dial. Self preservation kicked in and she prayed fervently that the man wouldn't answer.

"This is Viktor."

Damn. So much for prayer. Quickly she pushed the news past her lips and braced herself for his reaction, which never seemed to be what she expected. "I just received a meeting request from Sydni Cannes' personal secretary. I'm sure it'll be about the small electronics contracts."

"What are you going to tell her?"

"The same thing the pawn did when she asked him about it in passing, that it's simply a lag in accounting paperwork. By the time they figure it all out, we'll be long gone."

Silence.

Alex's lungs burned. Still, she was reluctant to release the breath frozen in her lungs. Viktor was so damn unpredictable. What was he going to say? Or do? Ruthless son of a bitch.

After a long pause, Viktor's deceptively soft and sexy voice drifted over the phone line.

"You play a dangerous game here, Alexandra." She opened her mouth to defend herself, but he brought her up short. "You know how turned on danger makes a man like me. In fact, just the thought of the possibility of getting caught has my dick so hard I could pound a hole in that sweet pussy of yours. So, get it over here. Now."

God, she was already in heat and practically

panting. Closing her eyes, she thought on the last time he'd fucked her into oblivion. The thickness of his cock had stretched her, pistoned into her body until her own cream frothed at her tight opening.

"I'd planned to go to lunch at Gervais-On-Vine. Meet me there instead? It's closer for a quickie..."

"No. Meet me at my office in twenty minutes. I'll tell my receptionist to expect you."

"Your place? I only have an hour, Viktor. Besides, why should I just jump when you say jump?" As if they hadn't covered this ground before.

"Darlin', you'll not only jump when I say, you'll pull out a trampoline to do so. Understand?"

Silence once again filled the line but his words set her pulse pounding. Alex closed her eyes again and Viktor's face appeared with such clarity if was as if she'd conjured him. The memory of his hands on her body, delivering such wicked pleasure...yeah, she'd do whatever he wanted, whenever and wherever he wanted it.

"And," he continued. "I don't care for that hoity-toity lunch spot you seem to enjoy. But if I send you there for the sole purpose of stripping naked and yodeling on the table, whether I'm there or not, you'll drop your drawers, get up on the bar and shake your ass for all you're worth. Then come to me, give me a report, and suck my cock until I tell you to stop. And you'll do it for two reasons—you're addicted to the fucking only I can give you. And you appreciate the seven million dollars you'll get in addition. Clear?"

"I'll see you in twenty minutes." The words came out all breath and need, but she didn't give a damn.

"Thought so," he said flatly.

Sigh. No wonder both her and the pawn were hooked on Viktor. The man played them so well.

Chapter Five

"Sydni, you're mumbling."

"Huh? Oh. Sorry. Something about the numbers on the purchase order report I was looking at earlier just don't make sense." She looked up from her chicken salad. Her heart skipped at least a couple of beats when Drew flashed a smile that totally reached his eyes. Sydni's concern about work leached right out of her bones and disappeared.

"Uh, I think I'll worry about it later," she said, staring at Drew so long she almost forgot to chew.

"Damn straight. Besides, you have a bet to fulfill and a hungry man to feed."

Oooh, and there went another twinkle in his crystalline gray gaze. The man was so good at double entendre. If they hung out long enough perhaps… Whoa. Back the hell up, Sydni. Keep it together girl.

But Drew was stroking the back of her hand, looking her dead in the eye with a hunger so blatant it set her pulse racing. Woo, just breathe, girl. Breathe.

"You have no shame, do you?" she asked him baldly, pulling her hand away. He wouldn't let go.

"None. Not an ounce. I told you yesterday that I intended to see you again. And again, and again."

"But why me? I mean, there are a ton of other women out there you could see, again and again." Just the thought made her sick but she squashed it down.

"If that was what I wanted, I'd be there. Now how about another bet?"

"Puh! I don't know. You made out like a bandit last time."

"I did, didn't I?" he chided. God, he was such a handsome man, built like a damn tank, yet so stylish he could grace the cover of the nearest billboard. In a word, he was a stunner. She still couldn't figure out what the hell he wanted with her. Self esteem was not an issue for Sydni...except when it came to dating. Former lovers had really pulled a few on her that left her jaded and a bit on the frosty side. Yet, something about Drew made her melt.

"So, since I made out like a bandit last time, you come up with the trivia question. I win, I get dinner and a chance to get to know you. Oh and endless kisses." He dipped his head and kissed her wrist. "You win, you get what you want."

"But I don't want anything." God, that sounded petulant. She rolled her eyes at herself. Drew must have thought she was rolling them at him.

"I'm sure you can think of something. But leaving you alone isn't an option. Not unless I really repulse you, Syd."

Crap. Why'd he have to go and say that? Drew didn't repulse her at all. In fact, the man intrigued her, attracted her. She'd just formed the thought in her head to say that if she won he'd find someone else to pester when he'd added that little caveat. Sydni'd always played by her own rules, set her own stage, yet something compelled her to let Drew define the pace of this game. Perhaps it was the fact that he'd just neatly plucked her only strategy right out of her hands.

"So what do you say, Syd?"

"Fine," she agreed, her brain hastily scrambling for the toughest movie trivia question she could think of. And just as hastily, she lost the bet. Again.

So why wasn't she more upset that she'd just, in essence, landed herself a boyfriend? One who was really looking forward to getting to know her.

In the biblical sense. "Oh shut up," she half-grinned, half-snarled to herself as the image of a off-balanced washing machine with her name plastered across the front of it popped into her mind. The man really did make her dizzy.

After lunch, Drew insisted on returning her to the exact spot he'd picked her up — her office. They strolled into Expedex, Inc. corporate headquarters, through the huge stainless steel and glass lobby and to the bank of shiny, silver elevators. The second the doors snicked closed, Drew hit the button for the eighteenth floor. And Sydni found herself backed against a mirrored wall, effectively caged between Drew's thick, cashmere-clad arms.

"Now," he growled. God, she loved the growly thing he did when he held her close. "I believe you owe me a kiss or five, Syd."

"What? Surely you weren't serious about that whole endless kiss thing?"

"Wrong. Serious doesn't begin to describe how I feel about you, woman."

"But you don't really know me," she protested breathily. Hell, it sounded pitiful even to her ears.

"But that's going to change, remember? Besides, I know plenty about you," he whispered, lowering his head until they were practically nose to nose. "You've taken care of your sister and put her through college. You're a successful woman with exquisite taste and style. You're strong, giving, smart, funny."

A light brush of soft lips over the skin just shy of her jaw sent a shiver vibrating across her collarbone.

"How can you know? I mean…"

"Just the fact that your sister thinks you're second only to God says plenty about the kind of person you are. I've been asking her to formally introduce us for a year. She moves a bit slow, that one."

Sydni laughed, then sucked in a breath as she got a whiff of not just his cologne, but the man's natural scent, just there at the crook of his neck. And when had he pulled her completely into his arms? More importantly, when had her feet moved to accommodate him?

Sydni's protests morphed into needy little whimpers when Drew proceeded to snatch the objection right out of her head with a kiss hot enough to make the nail polish on her toes liquefy. When he broke away, she was sucking wind, trying not to squirm from the zing shooting down between her thighs. It was enough to set her ablaze, make her want nothing more than the fulfillment of those endless kisses he'd finagled out of her.

"Dinner?" he suggested between nibbles and nips. Then he returned to his starting point, tasting her lip gloss in between short, panty breaths — mainly her short panty breaths..

Dinner? Why? They'd just had lunch. Besides, why bother with dinner when she could simply eat him up in four, well maybe six, big delicious bites. And Drew knew just how to work her. Knew which buttons to push. Knew how to make her want more of the sensuous mouth driving her wild.

Something dinged in the back of her mind. Duh — the elevator sounded for each floor it passed. Still, a few more levels to go. Plenty of time for her to chase his tongue from one edge of his yummy mouth to the other. All she needed was one more kiss. Yes, one more should do it. Wait, another. And another.

God, the feel, the taste of his lips on hers was like caramel and vanilla heaven. The arms wrapped around her body were unyielding, strong, made her feel safe and secure, yet so unsteady it was downright disconcerting—as if the elevator plunged straight down instead of heading up to the eighteenth floor.

This man who touched her so tenderly, yet boldly, made her feel more alive than she had in years, almost as if she were outside of herself. Suddenly the warmth of his body eased away. The spell entwined around her senses dissipated. Well, sort of.

Sydni's eyes remained closed, arms looped around his neck. Good gracious, get a-hold of yourself, Sydni. It's just a kiss and he's just a man. Right?

"Syd?"

"Huh?" Were those her words whooshing around like that?

"Dinner tomorrow night? I'll pick you up at seven sharp."

She was still trying to catch up to her lungs when the elevator doors slid open with a hiss. Drew shooed her out of the small space and out into the reception area. Gray eyes sparkled as the man watched her watching him through the shrinking space of the closing doors.

"Ms. Cannes, everything okay?"

Twirling around toward the voice, Sydni swallowed a surprised gasp at the knowing look on the receptionist's face. Pulling her wits about her, she nodded to the woman then marched down the hall to her private suite of offices wondering how Drew managed to roll right over her and get exactly what he wanted. And how in the world would she keep him from doing it again on their date tomorrow night? More importantly, did she even want to?

Drew headed out early, glanced at Sydni's car parked on the executive level as he passed by and recalled how she felt in his arms. During their cozy lunch this afternoon, the woman's nearness crawled underneath his skin and wiggled until there was no way he could resist kissing her. Thank god for winning that bet. She'd probably fall out if she knew he'd totally guessed the answer while his gut danced around with nervousness at the possibility of him guessing wrong.

Planning out his next moves with Sydni in his head, Drew headed straight to the shopping district, pulled into a swanky shop on designer row. Parking quickly he jumped out of his car. The receptionist, a pleasingly plump, gray haired woman dressed to the nines, greeted him as he entered the glass double doors of the establishment.

"Hi, Landy," he called with a wave.

"Hi yourself, handsome. Go on back. She's expecting you."

"Thanks."

The flirt blew him a kiss followed by a chuckle as he sent her one right back. After slipping into the new set of duds laid out in his personal dressing room, Drew headed into the fitting salon where Charli waited.

"So how was lunch?" Charli asked in a singsong voice.

She tucked a few pins into the cuffs of the pants he wore then folded them under.

"It was interesting. Your sister is going to be a tough catch. Stubborn."

Charli laughed heartily. "You have no idea. You up to the task?"

"Are you kidding me? I've been waiting for a chance like this since I saw her the first time at that soiree she threw for you when you launched the new business. I'm up to it, all right, Charli."

"Yep, my sister is as stubborn as a free-born mule. She's also convinced that all she needs is work, work, work." Charli left out the part about Sydni thinking Drew was simply too young for her. The man would just have to figure that one out on his own. And if Charli knew her handsome friend, he was exactly what Sydni needed — a man as stubborn and self-assured as herself. Charli bit the inside of her cheek to keep from cackling. God, she couldn't wait to see the fireworks when these two got together. Sydni wouldn't know what hit her! Hee hee! But there was one thing she needed to say first.

"Look, Drew, I know you've been bugging me for a long time to hook you up with my big sis. But in all honesty, the reason I didn't was because I've known you for years and I'm more than aware of the kind of women you're typically seen with."

Charli knew she had his attention when he stopped fidgeting with the waistband she was adjusting and went completely still.

"The kind of women I'm usually seen with? What do you mean, Charli?"

"I mean they're usually petite little perky blondes several years younger than the both of us. And my sister is anything but. I wasn't sure you were serious before."

"And now?" he asked, carefully, guarded.

"You've been bugging the hell out of me since you started working at the same company as her. All you talk about when we get together is Sydni. You ask about her. Wonder about her. Guess about her. And it seems you haven't dated in awhile. So I figured perhaps you were really serious."

"Hell, now that I see her all the time, all I can think about is her. I know she's not the type of woman I usually date, but I don't give a shit. I want her."

"For how long?" Charli asked pointedly.

"As long as she'll have me. The problem is getting her to the "have me" stage. I had to trick her into letting me stick around. Now I've got to figure out a way to keep her."

"Why her, Drew? I mean, why Syd? And if you tell me you've got a sudden thing for black women I'm going to kick your ass," Charli quipped.

"Everything about Syd, Charli." With that, heedless of the pins stuck in various places of his pants, he stepped down off the tailoring block and sat down in the nearest chair. Charli didn't think she'd ever seen Drew look more intense. Not even when they took the bar exam together.

"Charli, I swear, this isn't a simple fling for me. I'm old enough to know when someone has snagged my attention. Sydni not only snags it, she holds it. It was bad enough when I saw her at various functions with you. But now that I see her every day I find myself trying to run into her just so I can see her smile. To watch her walk. To hear her talk. To hear her speak with such confidence to her peers, then listen to her crack a corny joke and show her non-executive side. I don't even care which direction she's going and I'm trying to find a reason to follow her there. Her skin is perfect, flawless, smooth like Dove chocolate. Her hair is always pulled up into a classy knot on top of her head. I'd love to take it down and roll her long locs around my wrist and…ouch!"

Charli stuck him with a pin. "Okay, okay! More information than I needed to know, damn it!" she interrupted with a loud hearty laugh. "Now get your butt back up on the block so I can finish these pants and go take a cold shower."

Drew rubbed his thigh where she'd poked him, then hopped back up on the tailoring block.

"So where are you two going for your first dinner date?" Charli inquired.

"The Blue Ginger."

"Oooh, smart man. Nothing like Japanese gourmet to charm my sister."

"Then we'll take a little walk in the

arboretum under the moonlight. Hell, I've even checked the weather to make sure it'll be clear skies. And this time I managed to talk her into letting me pick her up."

"Why?" Charli wondered aloud.

"Because then I'll have to take her home. She'll either kiss me at the door or let me in to play."

They shared conspiratorial grins when Charli said, "You are a bad boy, Drew, and you don't play fair."

"Yeah I am, and no I don't."

Chapter Six

She'd been running on simmer since Drew picked her up this evening. The ambience of the restaurant he'd chosen would have been perfect if not for the butterflies that accompanied her main course. As Sydni enjoyed a traditional donburi pot, her stomach danced all over the place. And she almost lost a chopstick when Drew grinned up at her while he poured her another glass of wine. The man was dressed in a classy and elegant pair of navy blue trousers with a black long sleeved summer knit sweater. His dark hair was freshly cut and Sydni found herself wishing he'd left a bit more on the sides for her to run her fingers through. After all, she'd already agreed that they were in the "getting to know you" stage and Drew would kiss her later.

She wondered aloud at the golden hue of his skin. He answered without hesitation.

"My family is Sicilian on my father's side. My mother's family is from Spain. So we've all got the dark features. Hair, eyes, skin, the works."

And Sydni thought he was damn fine. She still couldn't believe she was sitting here with a man like Drew when she really should be at home working. Then the thought morphed into another one – working for what? Sure, she enjoyed her job, but it wasn't like she got brownie points for working herself to the bone. Hell, most folks didn't even know she spent most of her weekends pouring over numbers and putting together deals and proposals.

The truth of it? She was tired of dating men who thought it was normal to fuck her with their dress socks on—to stuffy to lay it on her the way she liked it. So full of themselves yet threatened by her, though she was a caring and giving person who could care less what they did for a living. They had no ambition, no drive. Were simply satisfied with the mediocre, yet tired of her quickly when they learned she'd risen higher in the ranks and made more money than they did. Or when they came over to dinner and acted like they couldn't touch anything because she lived in a better neighborhood than they did. Sydni was tired of landing idiots who felt they had to compete with her in order to love her. Or jackasses who felt they had to leave her for someone younger, women who were still making their way. So her solution had been to stop being bothered with them at all.

But Drew knew all these things about her and still wanted her? And speaking of age, their latest movie trivia question hit it dead on. The question—name the sixty-five year old actor who just had a child by his thirty-five-year-old wife. It made her teeth grate.

"Movie stars seem to do it all the time. I could name five actors off the top of my head that are dating or married to women twenty years their junior, or more," Sydni said as she looked up from her donburi pot. Her gaze went immediately to the working of Drew's throat as he took a sip of golden plum wine. She wasn't sure what was more potent, the drink or the man.

"You have something against younger lovers? I sense a story there," Drew said with a lazy, coaxing smile.

"Hmm, let me see," she snorted, one finger tapping her chin while her gaze rolled up to the ceiling. The perfect sarcastic pose. "My ex left me for a little pixie faced, barely blonde, loud mouthed chicklet almost fifteen years younger than me because I wasn't gullible and easily controlled. Well, he can have it. As for me, I don't date kids."

"Well, what do you consider a kid?"

Sydni suddenly felt like she was being backed into a corner, but for the life of her she couldn't stop her mouth from running.

"I think a man who goes for a woman fifteen years his junior is a damn lecher," she swore resolutely.

"Well, I'm in luck." At her tilted expression of confusion, Drew chuckled and said, "I'm only eight years younger than you, so that takes me firmly out of the kid category, and removes you from the lecher group."

Huh? Wait a minute. He hadn't been talking about male etiquette in dating younger women, but her stance on dating younger men? Holy shit! Smooth was the only word for him. But smooth didn't mean serious.

"Are you kidding me? You? And me?"

"Why not?" he replied, reaching across the table to take her by the hand. His index finger traced along her knuckles. Her gaze followed the manicured tips across her skin, imagined him traipsing those fingers along…Aw hell.

Back the hell up and focus, woman.

Forcing the sensual haze from her mind, Sydni left her hand in his but finally managed to pry her eyes away from his long, strong fingers. She met his gaze and the breath caught in her esophagus. The man's eyes pinned her with a predatory stare that made his beautiful gray eyes look like chipped ice. Not cold, but unyielding.

"But why me, Drew? I mean, look at you. You're brilliant, way manly gorgeous. And you even seem to have a pretty cool personality. What the hell could you possibly want with me?"

Drew scooted out of the booth, helped her up and led her toward the exit.

"Wait, the bill..."

"Already taken care of, beautiful. Come with me."

"To where," she gasped, making her high heels move faster as he towed her out the door.

"For a walk so I can answer your question in some semblance of privacy."

"What question?" Oh god, she was approaching delirious if she couldn't even remember what she'd asked him not three minutes ago.

"You asked why you. And I'm going to answer you. Thoroughly."

Oh. My. God. The man sucked all the air out of the sky and all the strength out of her typically stubborn resolve.

Next thing Sydni knew they were walking through the arboretum across the street from the restaurant. She knew this place intimately and the particular path he drew her down led to the middle of some lovely Japanese gardens with a bridge that stretched over a slow moving stream that reflected the glow of a full moon.

Oh-ho-ho the man was good and had no doubt planned this romantic interlude. And she'd stepped right into it and sank feet first.

"I've been wanting to meet you since Charli's big grand opening bash to christen her new designer tailor shop. I told you that before."

Crowding her against the railing, he planted a hand on either side of her hips, holding onto the metal and effectively caging her in.

But strangely, Sydni didn't feel trapped. She felt damn horny.

"Y-yes. I remember you saying that?"

He leaned closer.

"But I hadn't mentioned that I've been somewhat fascinated with you since the first time I saw you, and every time since then. Including every college function you accompanied Charli to. Every award ceremony. Her graduation. The celebration of her passing the bar exam."

So, uh, why hadn't she noticed him at any of those things? The answer — Charli had been the focus of her world. Charli and building her career. But now Charli was doing just fine and her career? Well, it was just fine too.

"But why? Why have you wanted to meet me?" She just had to know.

"Other than the fact that you're a beautiful woman, I want you for the same reasons you find me attractive, Sydni. You're classy. Solid and steadfast. Strong but feminine. In a word, perfect."

Then his lips were moving over hers. And god, could the man kiss. No guy this young should have such skill with his mouth. It made her wonder what else he was good at.

Her barely audible gasp must have been encouraging, because Drew had the nerve — god, she loved nerves — to deepen the kiss and press his body flush with hers. Oooh! The light bulb went on in her head. No wonder his perfectly fit trousers never showed evidence of what kind of package he carried. The man wore a cup! And whatever hid underneath it was dying to get out.

Did she really want to find out? Her body screamed "Yes!" but her common sense was having a problem. She'd just turned forty-two years old. What the hell was she doing out on a date with a man eight years younger?

Having fun, is what you're doing.

"Oh shut up," she muttered.

"Excuse me?"

"Not you, Drew. I'm talking to my damn conscience."

"Why? Is it telling you to drop your guard just a little bit and allow me a chance to make you happy?" He dropped a kiss into the hollow of her throat. "If it is, you should listen to it."

Strong teeth nipped the tendon between neck and shoulder, then sucked lightly on what happened to be a sweet spot. Sydni yelped then sighed, her arms slipping up and around his neck. His warm breath felt so good against her skin. His lips, even better.

"Mmm…"

"So, is that a yes, beautiful?" he whispered against her ear, taking advantage of the tilt of her head.

Oh god, yes. At her barely perceptible nod, he said, "Trust me, Syd, you won't regret it," then backed off just a little. Sydni was sure he'd meant to be reassuring by putting a bit of space between their bodies, but the mischief in his eyes belied the easy grace with which he moved. Boy, she was in so much trouble.

He held out a strong hand and waited for her to wrap her fingers around his. Then, hand in hand they continued across the bridge and along the boardwalk into god-knows-what.

* * * * *

After a car trip filled with lively music and even livelier conversation about the remakes of her favorite songs, Drew and Sydni strolled to her front door. And Sydni's feet were suddenly as cold at the Arctic Circle. She put her key in the lock but couldn't bring herself to turn around and face her new lover…whom she had yet to make love with.

There was no denying the serious chemistry between them. Well, she could deny it but that wouldn't make it go away. But out of control was never a feeling Sydni enjoyed, so it was time to grab the reins and pull this horse to a stop. Only, she couldn't quite face the man that she wanted to ride into oblivion.

Drew's scent wafted to her on the breeze, and it was all him. No funky cologne, no froo froo fragrance. Just Drew. Manly, musky and just-a-bit spicy Drew.

"Well, good night," she muttered with her

face practically wedged against the door jamb.

"Sydni?" he said softly. "Turn around, beautiful."

No way! If she faced him right now, she'd lose all her good sense and invite him inside to bump uglies all night. She'd never had sex on a first date. And hell, if she really thought about it, she'd hardly had what she'd call sex after entering a relationship, either.

Drew's hard body pressed in behind her. Strong hands eased up and down the goose flesh on her arms, skillfully kneading the muscles of her biceps and shoulders. Warm and sure, yet gentle.

"Sydni, look at me," he insisted, turning her with a gentle nudge.

Taking her chin firmly in hand Drew moved in for a kiss so soul stirring and deep it reached clear to the tips of her freshly pedicured toes and made them curl against the inside of her kitten heeled sandals. Moving his mouth over hers, the man plundered, took, pushed passed the natural barrier of her lips and tangled his tongue with hers. There was no gentle coaxing, nothing of what she expected. This was a claiming of territory, a branding of the senses. It was impossible not to respond.

No man had ever jumped in with both feet like Drew. Had ever kissed the wind out of her sails as if he had a right to her. And damn, it was sexy.

Next thing she knew, her fingers were busy wrinkling the front of his sweater as she tipped her head back to give him better access to that spot near her shoulder that made her squirm. The second her head tilted, he bit down.

"Aaah. God," she sighed. So he did it again. And again.

The pouty lips of her sex ached, plump and swollen with need. And Sydni's favorite underwear were certainly good for nothing now, given how the wet fabric was plastered against the flesh of her trimmed mound.

Drew's biceps and forearms flexed like steel rope coiled underneath his skin as one arm held Sydni tight and the other eased down her body to play along her ribs. His breathy groan brought her back to reality long enough to realize they were standing on her porch underneath a bright-as-hell light triggered by motion detectors. And there was definitely enough motion between them to make the stupid thing come on.

Sydni opened her eyes, squinted against the

brightness and took a step back. He followed. Another step had her ass plastered against the front door while gorgeously sculpted pecs smashed across her front. They both had pebble hard nipples, only his were accompanied by a broad expanse of chest. Dayum!

"Are you going to invite me in?" he crooned. Before Sydni could answer Drew was on her again. This time a series of gentle brushes beneath the swell of a breast had Sydni practically gasping. Another touch just below her puckered sensitive areola, followed by a controlled pinch sent her into a tailspin of lust.

Tomorrow would be soon enough to worry about what she'd gotten herself into. Tonight, she was going to get a much needed fuck. Glad I'm on the Pill. The thought just popped into her head all on it's on. Well, actually Drew's proximity to her person no doubt helped it along, but that wasn't the point. Besides, she was only on the Pill to keep her periods light and on schedule…not that she really kept up with the things since she had no prospects. Wait, that wasn't true anymore, was it? She had a big, dark haired determined prospect standing right in front of her.

Not bothering to answer Drew's question,

Sydni opened the door, grabbed him by the hand and shut it firmly behind her. The high heels went flying as she kicked them off in the foyer. Drew took a quick look around the tiled foyer and the open French doors of her office off to the left. The open floor plan allowed him to see past the wide entry way where two sets of curved stair cases led upstairs. Past the stairs was a sunken family room with a formal dining room off to one side and a gourmet kitchen, complete with granite and stainless steel everything, off to the other.

Sydni liked being able to see the entire expanse of the huge first floor. Then Drew gave her another reason to appreciate the lack of dividing walls. He dropped his jacket at the door, followed by his belt and pants. His shirt and underwear left a trail across the hardwood floors on his way to the family room. Once there, the man flopped his naked ass down on her chaise lounge, and held his hand out to her with an expectant come-hither half-grin across his lips. One foot planted on the floor gave an excellent view of a stiff, fat cock that reached for her in more ways than one.

Breath stuck in the lungs of an amazed Sydni who stood rooted to the spot at the front door, not missing one little bit of the view. My god, Drew was more delicious than she'd believed. He was all perfected, sun kissed gold. A dusting of hair on his chest was as dark as the hair on his head. The build of his thighs said he did lots of squats, and the individual muscles of his quads were visible without him even having to flex them.

Sydni looked down at the pile of clothes he'd discarded at her bare feet. A sports cup lay on top of his boxers a few feet away. And now she knew what he'd hidden behind that bit of plastic — a cock so mouthwatering and thickly veined she found herself licking her lips. It was wide, but not overly long and would surely stretch her deliciously. It pulsed with life, a true golden rod so engorged the fat head was a mottled purple, like a ripening plum. Sydni wondered what he tasted like.

"Keep looking at me like that, Sydni, and you won't make it in here to the couch," he growled, obviously trying to give her the opportunity to undress herself at her own pace. Then again, maybe she didn't want to undress herself at all.

Teeth worried her lower lip as her eyes continued to rake up and down Drew's lovely body as he sat half-reclined in the family room. Sydni leaned back against the front door, eased her skirt up around her waist and proceeded to surprise herself. Easing the scrap of useless underwear to the side, fingers pressed into her own heated flesh. Her gaze never left Drew's. Sydni had never touched herself in front of a man. Hell, that was their job, right?

Well, not tonight. Tonight she felt sensual, sexy and completely uninhibited. Her head thunked against the door as her fingers smeared over her throbbing clit as she watched Drew's glorious cock bob uncontrollably.

One second she was imagining the slide of that piece of pleasure against her soaked core. The next second Drew was up off the couch, his long legs eating up the distance between them, cock waving all the while. In the foyer he swung her into his arms and took off running. And he was right—she never made it to the couch.

Allowing Sydni to undress herself had been his way of backing off a bit, giving her the space to come to him freely, or say no if she felt the need.

The second her fingers disappeared in her pussy, Drew's resolve snapped like a dry twig in winter. His heart rate kicked up and the rod of his cock, which was solidly erect before, became downright painful. When she pulled her fingers out before plunging them back inside what he knew was going to be honeyed heaven, a groan ripped its way past his throat at the slick essence all over her hand. More than ready for him. And he needed inside more than he needed air to breathe.

The office was the perfect spot. Not to mention, the closest.

He set Sydni on the edge of her desk and eyeballed the drenched fingers now disappearing into her mouth. Drew watched her luscious lips wrap around them, shuddered at the murmured appreciation of her own taste echoing in the air.

Suddenly, she was a siren. Her beautiful brown eyes bored into his gray ones as she spread her legs wide. Her tongue left a wet trail over her top lip while full round hips rolled with bold invitation. Other than the most primal and basest impulses, Drew's brain and common sense shut down. He was all instinct, passion and lust.

God, the woman had him so turned around he'd be searching for the slightest glimpse of her with a flashlight in the daytime.

Stepping close Drew's head fell back on his shoulders when the head of his cock brushed up against her soaked heat. Then ground his stiff cock against her mound. Mmm, that felt good.

"First date. No real sex," she sighed brokenly. A sexy little shiver slithered up her body.

"Not our first date," he murmured. "Third one."

"Details, details. The lawyer in you is showing," she gasped. And he was right if lunch counted as dates number one and two. There was no doubt she wanted him, but couldn't quite move past the cooling apprehension slithering around at the base of her belly. Sure she could put a hurtin' on a man, make him beg for more. But it had been so long, a Drew was so young. What if she couldn't keep up, didn't please him? And worse, what if he actually had no "skillz" and didn't please her?

Sinking to his knees, Drew took the reins out of her control. A hand landed in the middle of her chest and gently pushed until Sydni's back met the cool wood desk.

"Let me taste you. God, Syd, you're so fucking sexy, and so luscious I just want to go diving. Right here," he growled, sinking a single finger into her soaked heat.

An agile tongue flicked across her clit with alternating licks along her slit and an occasional dip into her hole. Wet warmth passed over the puckered entrance of her ass and sent her back bowing up off the desk with the pleasure. God, the man was everywhere.

Legs pushed apart as far as they would go, Drew proceeded to lick, suck and nibble her into orgasm number one. Every moan and growl originated from her clit and zoomed clear to her scalp, making her curly hair even curlier while she humped his face like a woman riding a bucking bronco. And boy was she ever rewarded for her troubles.

When home alone, Sydni always switched off her toy of the moment after orgasm number one and slipped into a coma-like sleep. But Drew pushed her past what she'd always believed was her limit. He lapped and tongued her headlong into another orgasm that had her stomach muscles clenching wildly and her thighs fighting to press together though a wide set of shoulders aided his strong arms in keeping them spread wide.

Oh god, she simply couldn't take anymore.

Sitting up to push against his head she pried him away from her soaked core and scooted off the desk.

"Enough." Hell, anymore and she'd become a total addict, complete with slobbering stupor and all. "My turn," she declared, then pushed him back and off before tumbling them to the carpet. Sydni raised a single black brow and flashed an impish grin then delivered a round of decadent kisses down his torso.

"Ah, a take charge woman, eh? Don't get used to it, baby."

Drew wasn't usually the type to be dominated during sex. If anything, it was the exact opposite. But he'd let her get away with it. This time.

And when her warm mouth slammed down over his throbbing cock, Drew's back spasmed up off the thick carpet in tandem with a loud yell. My god! The woman gave him no warning. No preliminary, tentative or coy licks. No, she simply swallowed him in one big gulp and took him clear to the back of her throat.

A fingertip tapped gently as the spot just behind his balls as her mouth gobbled him down…and up, and down. And up.

"Shit! My god, woman, you're an expert," he

gasped.

"Mmm hmm," she crooned. Drew heard the smile in her voice.

Sydni sucked him like he was her favorite pastime. Her favorite dessert. Her favorite everything. Easy suction accompanied the swirl of warm wet tongue over his flesh. She took a pass over the engorged head, then another that sent a bolt of energy flashing through his hard length and clear to his sac. That last nibble was accompanied with just a little bit of friction from her sharp teeth followed by a hard suck. Her tongue did wonders over the head of his cock. And the traitorous thing gave only a split second of warning before it exploded with jet after jet of sticky cum right down her throat.

Not a single drop escaped her voracious licking. Wow.

But he should have been mortified. An orgasm hadn't succeeded in escaping his control since his college days. Yet this sweet morsel of a woman had managed to strip him. And damn if he cared, especially since Sydni was, and would remain, the only woman who had this kind of power over him. He would see to it.

She raised her head after one final lick. "Mmm, you taste so sweet. How?"

Drew flipped them over until he was on top, then kissed the tip of Sydni's nose while his hands explored her lovely body. He grinned down at her, never letting up on the pressure he forced on her sensitive nipples. One hand drifted lower to tickle the crease at her groin.

"Pineapple juice," he whispered against her ear as his teeth played with her earring.

"Pine…oh, god," the words faded as her voice gave way to a deep moan when his fingers slid deep.

"I'd hoped to find myself in this position, literally. So I drank a lot of pineapple juice the last couple of days. Wanted my cum nice and sweet, just for you."

Drew's recovery time was about twenty minutes. So he'd just have to keep her busy until then. And there was nothing like teasing and suckling Bing cherry nipples. Sydni's moans and urgent movement soon made his cock stir to life against his groin. The weeping head sat up and looked around for a succulent channel to occupy.

And Sydni's sex was just as fragrant and enticing as the fruit he'd eaten for the past couple of days. Juicy and cocoa-pink he couldn't wait to sink himself into her creaming channel.

"Bedroom. Quick," she gasped with need.

Drew picked her up, glad when she automatically wrapped her legs around his waist as he flew toward the stairs.

The carpet was thick and soft under his bare feet as he navigated the left staircase. Gritting his teeth against the delicious friction of his cock against her dewy center, he headed in the direction Sydni indicated between her sweet moans and gasps.

The woman had style. Everything up here was done in tans, golds, winter white and rich burgundy. But damn he wished her house was just a bit smaller so he could get her to a bed faster. The feel of her warm skin sliding against his almost made him stop at the nearest wall and pushing her up against it to take her hard and fast.

"Last door on the left. Oh god, hurry!"

Once in her bedroom, Drew didn't bother to look around. All he wanted was the bed with Syndi spread over it.

"Nightstand drawer," she gasped with a wild roll of her hips. "Condom."

He reached over, slid open the drawer and blindly groped for a little foil packet, handed it to Sydni as he sank back on his knees between her thighs.

She sat up with her legs draped over his thighs and snatched the condom out of his fingers. The woman was quick, flexible and agile. Perfect combination for hot jungle sex. Damn. All it did was make him hotter.

"Sydni, I want inside of you, baby. I've never had unprotected sex with a woman. My last trip to the doctor was thankfully uneventful and I haven't been with anyone since then."

Panting, still struggling with the stupid condom, she asked, "How long?"

"A year."

Her expression said, "Yeah right," but her lips simply trembled as he fingered her clit. Sydni rolled the condom over his thick stalk. It broke.

Drew grabbed another little packet. Her hand shook as she tried to open it and slide it over his girth. He winced—it was just too small. He grimaced at the pain of the thing squeezing his cock like a rubber band wrapped too tight over a finger. Finally, the damn rubber ripped.

"Syd, I'm clean but I have more condoms in my wallet." Ones that fit, he thought as one hand worked her breasts and the other sank two fingers deep into her quivering sex. "I can go downstairs and get one."

She gathered up the ruined condoms and tossed them into the air yelling desperately, "Oh god, just fuck me already! Please."

First date, or second date…hell, some rules were made to be broken.

Fingers dug into Drew's biceps as he eased inside, pulled back, then pushed in a bit more. Breath forced itself from her lungs in wrenching gasps. Such pleasure. Such mind numbing, nerve tingling pleasure.

Scalding delicious thickness stretched her to just below the burning point. Sydni was sure she'd never taken anything quite so thick, but wanted more of it anyway.

And then he was seated. A lover's kiss, so tender and sweet bombarded her senses with the taste, the smell of him. Mmm, her own scent was mixed in from when he'd gone down on her. Then his large hand landed on her hip with a smack. She yelped, then yelled as the man began to work her pussy like a specially designed snow plow blowing everything out of its way leaving the smooth evidence of its passing for days to come. Ass muscles bunched as Drew worked his length in and out of her body. A deep exhale and an oh-so-manly grunt accompanied each full thrust. Her thighs trembled and burned as he fucked her deep, then deeper still. And all she could think was, "More".

And for goodness sake, he accommodated her until she exploded again. Three orgasms in one go-round? It was unheard of. Impossible.

Sigh…

Fucking wonderful.

A couple of hours later, Drew awoke with the hard-on from hell. Well, no wonder — his groin was pressed into the perfect crease of Sydni's sweet and wonderfully bare ass. Unable to resist, he dipped his head and nibbled the soft skin on the back of her neck until she squirmed.

Stretching with a sigh and a lopsided grin, the woman rolled over and looked up at him with the most satisfied expression. God, would he love to see her rouse from sleep with this same look on her face every morning.

He'd admired Sydni from a distance, simply taken aback by her no matter where he spotted her — like at the function to celebrate Charli's making the national honor society while in law school her second year. Then Charli's graduation. Charli's launch of her new career as clothes diva extraordinaire to the stars.

Everything had been about Charli. Even Charli was tired of being the center of Sydni's attention. Well, guilty was more like it. Sydni's sister wanted nothing more than for her to be happy and believed there was no time like the present considering how long Syd had taken care of everything and everyone else.

Yep, now it was Sydni's time to see to herself. Or, rather, Drew's time to see to her.

He just hoped she felt the same tomorrow.

Speaking of tomorrow, he'd better get going.

"Thank you for a wonderful evening, gorgeous. I'd better get going. I start a new position in the morning. I should probably get home and get some sleep."

"You're leaving Expedex?" The alarm on her face told him she'd miss him if he did.

"No. I'm being promoted. But it's nice to know you'd care whether I left or not."

"Well, of course I'd care," she grumped and looked away shyly.

Drew lowered his head and placed a quick peck on Sydni's forehead. And that simple peck took wing and turned into a soul-stirring lip lock that made his ass muscles twitch.

Sydni's warm hand slid between their bodies and wrapped around his cock.

"Before you leave, how 'bout some good luck lovin' for your new job tomorrow?"

Sydni didn't give him a chance to agree, simply climbed on top of him and slid her warm, tight sex over his cock. In seconds Drew was seated to the hilt inside of her welcoming body. When she started to move her talented hips, Drew sat up, crossed his legs underneath her lush ass and took hold of her firm cheeks. Latching onto a nipple he suckled a firm berry and bounced her up and down on his rod until he felt the first ripples of her sleek inner muscles.

Tapping her clit he said, "Lunch tomorrow?"

"How am I supposed to think at a time like this?" she panted, head thrown back.

"Think fast," he ground out, surging forward and earning a sensual shriek from his lover.

"I've never been the submissive type, you bossy bastard." Another deep lunge of Drew's cock and she panted like a winded runner.

"Sure you have, beautiful. You were just waiting for me to bring it out of you. A man you can trust enough to really let go. Outside the bedroom, you're the boss. Inside this room, that job's mine. Starting right now, so…" He licked her ear and did that growly thing that sent a current of lust zinging through her cells.

"Answer my question, Syd."

Another hard delicious dig followed by several shallow thrusts.

"What question? Oh god, Drew," Sydni pleaded. "I need to cum. Please."

"Lunch tomorrow?"

"Yes!" she yelled.

Speeding up his movements, Drew gritted his teeth, determined she would drench his cock in the next few strokes.

"Damn, Syd. I love being inside you. Come for me. Give it to me, baby."

Her compliance was immediate, fervent...and loud.

Chapter Seven

Feeling antsy for no apparent reason, Sydni joined her colleagues around the conference room table. All of the senior execs had arrived and the only person missing was her boss, the CEO of Expedex. Ten minutes later, the tardy exec walked in followed by a perfectly tailored suit that covered a body Sydni had come to know all too well just last night.

Drew?

"I'd like to introduce a new addition to our executive legal team, Mr. Drew Caruth. He's being promoted to Senior Counsel and will assist the lead attorney in our Japanese division with the expectation of taking it over after he gets comfortable in a few months. As with all our attorneys, he will continue to report to Mr. Schaff, the Chief Legal Advisor, but is assigned exclusively to Ms. Cannes division."

Sydni bit the inside of her cheek to keep from gasping aloud, but it came out a gurgled sigh anyway. All eyes swung her direction. With a practiced bland expression firmly in place, she tapped her pen against her cheek and pretended to be deep in thought, before further pretending to take notes on the legal pad sitting on the table in front of her.

The old bastard looked directly at Sydni and said, "Ms. Cannes, thank you in advance for helping with Drew's transition. I'm sure you'll get on well together. Now on to other business..."

All the while, her insides squirmed like a worm on a hook. Why the Japanese division? That was her division, damn it. She might be Executive Vice President of International Shipping for Japan, and not responsible for the legal division, but it still felt like Drew was encroaching on her territory, the bastard. Besides, she'd been working with the lead attorney on contracts and proposal for years. Now she'd have to break in a newbie? And it wasn't just any newbie. It was someone she'd slept with. Well, fucked was more like it considering they got very little sleep when Drew had been over at her house. Correction, used to come to her house. After today, she wasn't sure he was welcome anymore.

Why hadn't the man mentioned his promotion meant coming to her side of the organization?

Ignoring Drew as he sat across the table from her, Sydni pushed away her irritation and zoned in on the upcoming projects and business issues. The second the meeting was over she slipped out the door and marched straight back to her office while everyone else welcomed the new guy on the team.

Instructing her receptionist to hold her calls, Sydni ensconced herself behind closed doors and tried to concentrate on the details of yet another contract to ship electronics from Japan.

Unbidden, an image appeared of Drew leaning down over her as she sat at her desk pointing out details on this deal or that contract. Then pressing into her back, getting close enough for her to catch his scent. Then closer still until she felt his pecs, warmth seeping through his shirt and into her skin. She blinked and tried to calm the rush of heat suffusing her body.

A frustrated groan left her throat when she closed her eyes again, and there were his lips slowly approaching to nibble the sweet spot on her neck.

Shit.

Her lids snapped open as her memory brought to mind why she was supposed to be mad at the man. They'd fucked like bunnies yet he hadn't managed to mention he would be working directly with her from now on? In her fucking division. In fact, if she wasn't mistaken, he'd be no more than an office or two down the hall. So what if she wasn't actually his boss. That wasn't the goddamn point.

The intercom quietly beeped.

"Sore wa Cannes Sydni des. Hello, this is Sydni Cannes."

"Mr. Caruth is here to see you, ma'am."

"Thank you, Tsubaki-san. Send him in," she replied politely. "And please hold all calls and appointments for the rest of the day."

"Yes, ma'am."

She placed the phone on the cradle just as Drew stepped in looking like sin on wheels. Just perfect, 'cause she felt like a bitch on heels.

"Wanna tell me what the hell you're doing in my division?"

The man had the nerve to tilt his head and look at her like she was crazy. Sydni didn't give a shit. He may be the man in bed. But 'round here, she was the woman.

"Nice to see you too, Syd." His fingers tapped the deadbolt and the sound of the lock snicking into place sent the fine hairs on the back of Sydni's neck into hyper disco mode.

"I didn't come in here to argue. You promised me lunch today."

"That was before you deceived me, damn it."

"Deceived you? What did I lie about, Syd? I did mention my promotion, I just didn't mention moving into your space. Why? Because I'm not going to have my woman thinking I want to be with her so she can get me a fucking job." Jaw ticking and color rising in his cheeks, Drew quietly snapped every word through gritted teeth. The man was actually mad? Now didn't that beat all? Snark!

Whoa! His woman? Was he serious?

"I never want you to feel used or taken for granted, Syd. I want you to feel cherished while I give you the ride of your life. You deserve to be happy, baby. And if I'm not man enough to make my own way, there's no way I'm man enough to keep you."

Hell, just take all the heat out of my mad, why dontcha.

Unfolding his arms from across his wide chest, his stance was a bit more relaxed, thank god. Drew alone was enough. Drew plus intense pissed off male was too explosive by half. Well, at least he didn't seem the type to hold a grudge.

"So, where would you like to go?" he asked with a come-hither tilt of his head.

"I don't have time for lunch."

"How about a nice hard fuck, then I bring you back something to eat after I've had my fill of you?"

"Huh?" Oh how articulate, Sydni. God, she wanted to kick herself at how easily he reduced her to a blithering dimwit.

"You didn't think last night was a one night stand did you?"

"I-I, uh…" In fact, she'd wondered, but had been so exhausted by the time he left her early this morning, she hadn't had the wits to catch him and have "the talk" about where this all was going.

But now the man was closer than arms length and moving in fast. A full-body shudder worked its way through Sydni's nervous system when an open mouthed lick traveled up her neck, followed by Drew sucking on her earlobe, diamond stud and all.

"I…oh, dear god. I'm sorry," she stammered. "I just don't have time to go anywhere today. Something's come up." Yes, work. Work had always been her safe haven. She could hide any... Hold up. She wasn't hiding from Drew, was she?

"Of course you have time," he sighed into her ear, then bit that damn spot that made her insides dance an Irish jig as if she were the lead in the cast of Riverdance. "Fucking is like Jell-O. There's always room for Jell-O." And his voice did that growly thing she liked. Yep, for a woman who'd always been ruled by her intellect and drive to succeed, the man reduced her to a shivering mass of lust and need with little more than a nip or two. In a word, she was toast. Burnt. No butter.

Her seat twirled around to face him. Drew wasted no time hitting his knees and pushing hers apart. Why, oh why hadn't she worn her granny panties and control top hose instead of sheer thigh-highs today? Because when you got up this morning you recalled a sexy night in Drew's arms and felt all siren-delicious.

Well, thigh-highs meant there was nothing between Drew and her creaming pussy but a scrap of fabric that barely passed as underwear. If the sight of her old-stand-by drawers hadn't discouraged him away, then he would have at least had to work at getting the panty hose off.

"Oh shit!" Sydni clamped down on her

bottom lip when his fingers eased the crotch of her barely there undies aside. He dove right in with a lick from the bottom of her already creaming slit to the top, his tongue lodged just underneath her hooded clit.

"Oh my god, stop. Tsubaki-san will come running thinking something is wrong."

He lifted his head with an imp of a smile. "Then you'll just have to be quiet, won't you?"

"Bastard," she hissed.

"Damn right."

Talented tongue and even more talented fingers had her humping his face like a nympho on cock-flavored crack.

One hand aided his mouth in tormenting her while the other eased down her thighs, caressed the back of her knees, then slid down to the top of the ankle boots she decided to sport today. When she'd stepped into them this morning, she had to admit to herself that she'd indeed been thinking of this man.

"Damn, these are some sexy shoes. Shoes made just for fucking. Mmmm." He nipped the swollen bud of her clit and said, "The way the tops zip up to hug your ankles so tight reminds me of the way your sweet pussy wraps around my cock. Well, let's put those boots to use, shall we?"

What? Put them to use?

"Stand up, Syd. I'd be totally wrong not to fuck you when you're wearing such a sexy assed pair of fuck-me boots."

She loved high heels, loved the way they made her long legs look even longer, her calves more streamlined and sleek. And this particular pair just seemed to ooze sex as she'd modeled in front of her mirror this morning with nothing on but her stockings, bra and these, as Drew called them, 'fucking shoes'.

He nibbled and sucked on her lower lips for a few seconds more, then scooted back and stood, holding out his hand. The second her fingers met Drew's, he eased her up and around so she stood with her hands on her desk facing the door — the door that reminded her someone could be just on the other side.

This was crazy! And her ability to conjure up the least bit of care was strangely missing. The alarm she expected to come running into her head never appeared. Finally, she managed to take enough breaths to get some semblance of sanity back. But it was a close thing.

Pushing away from her desk Sydni attempted to right her clothing. Yuck. Her underwear was cold against her heated flesh when she settled them back into place. "Drew, look, I-we can't do this here. It's just not a good…"

And just like that her shirt was unbuttoned and whisked off, followed by her bra. At least he'd had the sense to hang her blouse neatly over the back of the chair that was soon kicked off to the side. Sydni was settled over the cool wood of her desk, breasts smashed against the calendar that covered the smooth polished top, and her skirt hiked up around her waist. The panties disappeared altogether and Drew's hands made trails all over her silky stockings.

"The privileges of being an Executive VP. Your door is locked. Don't think, baby. Just feel." The seductive words were followed by a smack to her bare ass that sent a startled expression to her face and a zing to her pussy. The damn thing creamed ridiculously while he knelt again and licked her like a lollypop. Now it produced enough dew to supply the entire nation with enough cream for a year.

She went to stand up. Strong fingers pressed into the middle of her back until her chest was once again flat against the cool finish of the desk.

"Head down. Ass up."

Smack!

Oooh, god. It was just too wrong for a man this young to have skills this polished. What the hell had happened? Sydni had always dominated in the sex department. Well, it was obvious Drew wasn't having it. And to her surprise, she liked it.

"Mmm, your ass is so nice and round."

Smack!

His big hands soothed the slight sting, slid up her back and around her shoulders, caressing the skin, easing along until his fingers tugged and rolled her nipples, making her hips roll right along with them.

"Damn, baby, I love your body."

"Puh," she snorted. "Flattery much? Knowing my hips are too wide and my ass is too big."

"If I wanted a Barbie doll, I would have pursued one. You're perfectly lush and curvy in all the right places. I love holding your ass in my hands while I fuck you. And I don't have to be afraid of breaking you."

Her entire being heated in anticipation. God she wanted him.

The plump head of his cock nudged against her achy center. Slippery and slick with dew,

Sydni wiggled frantically trying to get him inside knowing he would stretch her just to the burning point exactly the way she liked.

In one smooth thrust, he sank deep with a quiet hiss. "I've always wanted to be able to let go with a woman. Fuck like an animal. Let the wild man out that I have to keep hidden underneath a suit and tie during the day. Now finger your clit while I slide deep into your wet pussy."

The silk of his shirt tickled the skin on her back. One of the buttons dug into her spine as Drew pressed against her body, whispering in her ear. He'd almost slid free but the head of his cock caught the tight ring of her sex and was held fast by the flexing muscles. An orgasm of cosmic proportions hovered just out of reach, and god she wanted it. Wanted it until every cell in her nervous system screamed for it. Craved it.

"I can give it to you like you want it, like you need it, Syd. Do you need it, baby?"

Did she ever! Yet all he delivered was the very tip of his cock rimming her drenched gate, teasing her relentlessly.

His cock flexed and set off a vibration deep inside her spasming channel. Breath warm against her cheek, he said, "If you want it, tell me how much."

"I want it," she started to scream, then bit down on her lip remembering she was bare-assed across her office desk covered by a man who was perfection wrapped in smooth peaches-and-cream skin. And his cock was addictive, thick, pulsing with life. And evidently he was intent on making sure she understood she was all his.

"Oh god, Drew. Fuck me, please. More."

He surged forward. She yelped, then bit her bottom lip again — at this rate the thing would be swollen for sure when this was over. Well, she'd just have to give him a fat lip to match hers for driving her crazy like this. When buried all the way inside, the tip of his staff tapped the entrance to her womb. Thick and long, he stretched her deliciously, hovering just on the edge of too much. A perfect fit.

"Is this what my baby needs?" he crooned. A warm wisp of breath tickled the fine hairs on the column of her neck.

"Oh god, yes. That's it, Drew. Right there."

"Feel good, baby?"

"Yes. God, yes. Feels sooo good."

"Come for me, Syd. Cream my cock."

Sydni became a babbling idiot. There was no way it could be helped. The man made her feel like a goddess. A nasty, uninhibited, fuck-a-holic goddess. Then reduced her to a needy puddle of horny, liquid, satisfied woman.

Mouth open on a silent scream, Sydni's thighs trembled to the same cadence as her orgasm as she exploded around the lovely pole reaming her. Squeezing her eyes tight enough to see stars she held onto her desk for dear life. If she let go at the same time Drew pulled away from her, she'd end up sprawled on the thick carpeted floor for sure.

Then he flexed that perfect monster of a cock inside her and filled her with his cream. Untamed, growly groans filled her ear as he hissed the words that set her heart racing.

"Damn, I'm coming Syd. I just can't resist you, woman. And you're all mine."

Hauled up against his side, Drew shuffled Sydni into the small private bathroom and sat her on top of the vanity. With sure but gentle strokes, he lovingly washed her up against all her protesting and batting hands. He even helped her touch up her makeup, what little she wore anyway.

Talented lawyer. Excellent lover. Seemed to be a genuinely nice guy too. So, what the hell was he doing with her? Sure she was nice to look at, kept in as good a shape as she could given the demands of her job. A successful business woman with her own way and means. Nice house—Charli called it a museum—in a nice part of town. And most important, other than her house, she was completely debt free.

But she was forty-fucking-two years old. Considering she wasn't looking to start a family or have kids of her own, why was somebody like Drew hounding her?

"Syd, you're thinking too hard again."

Yeah, she tended to do that a lot in his company. He gave her a peck on her cheek and helped her down from the counter top.

"I think we're as fresh as we're gonna get. How 'bout lunch in the cafeteria?"

"Drew I can't."

"You need to eat, Sydni. It's unhealthy. I won't take no for an answer."

"God, you're a bossy something or other."

He flashed a million-dollar-baby smile that lit up the bathroom.

"Glad you think so. Now let's get a bite."

"Fine. I'll meet you downstairs in a few

minutes."

"Sydni," he drawled with exasperation.

"I won't stand you up. I just need to handle a couple of things and I'll be there. Promise."

With a wink and another cheek peck, he turned and left the bathroom. And Sydni stood in the mirror and fanned herself. The man was H-O-T- hot! Enough to melt the tile under her feet.

But still…he had no need for a sugar mama. So what the hell did Drew Caruth really want? Other than mind blowing sex, of course. Sydni pondered all the way down to the company's gourmet restaurant on the tenth floor. Thought about it until Drew caught her attention and pinned her with a riveting, gray, I-want-you gaze. Sigh.

* * * * *

Alex watched from her favorite spot in the cafeteria. On days when she wasn't summoned to Viktor's office, house, or car for a mid-afternoon horny session, she people-watched here in the Expedex employee lounge, which was more like a four-star restaurant. And today, her people of choice were Sydni Cannes and her new lawyer stud. Nobody told her that the new guy and Sydni were lovers. Nobody had to. If there was one thing Alex was good at, was reading the body language of a sexually satisfied woman.

Perhaps she could use their association to her advantage?

"Viktor, it's Alex," she spoke quietly into the mouthpiece of her phone.

"What?"

"I think I may see a way to get Cannes to drop her little investigation of the contracts."

"You're a smart woman. Handle it."

"Right. And what about the pawn? Does he know what to do?"

"I only fuck him, Alex. I'm leaving the rest up to you."

She grimaced. God, she hated his condescending, self-righteous attitude. She was trying to save his ass here, and he had the nerve to get stupid and lay it all in her lap?

"Big deal," she snarled into the handset. "I fuck him too. Does that mean I should pass this all back to you?" Asshole.

Silence. Followed by a quiet baritone, menacing and smooth. "Are you getting smart with me, Alexandra?"

A shiver worked its way into the bones of her spine. Her mind raced with all kinds of retorts. But her mouth proved it was currently smarter than her brain and stayed shut. "You are there. I am not. Do whatever you think you need to do with Cannes and the pawn. And…" He paused. Never a good sign. "I'll see to you later, as always."

Instantly, she creamed as every nerve ending tingled in anticipation of what he would do to "see to her". God, the man was so good at being bad.

"Be at my house at six thirty this evening. Wear that lined leather trench coat I gave you last month. With nothing else. And Alex?"

"Yes?"

"Come prepared to serve."

"A-all right." Breathless and just a little bit afraid, the words barely made it through the mouthpiece of the phone. Alex squeezed her thighs together and tried to ignore the way that being in the dark about what Viktor planned to set her pulse racing and her cunt creaming. He was a sick bastard. And she loved it. So what did that make her? "Wait, Viktor, I'm supposed to see the pawn tonight."

"Expect him to call and break his date with you. I'll be seeing him earlier. While he's asleep in my bed, you will do your penance wherever I choose."

"Yes. Okay."

She waited until Viktor disconnected the call then snapped her own phone closed. Alex cast a quick glance across the expanse of the dining area to where Miss High-And-Mighty executive Cannes sat with her new gorgeous pet. A smile spread across her face as she tossed her trash in the receptacle and headed out the door. And just that quickly a plan formed into a solid wall of sheer will in her head.

Chapter Eight

The last few weeks had been heaven and thankfully predictable. Sydni knew Drew waited in the cafeteria in the same spot they'd been meeting everyday. He was settling into his new position at Expedex quite nicely. Not to mention settling into her just as nicely.

The intercom beeped, and Tsubaki-san's soft voice came through. "Miss Charli on line one to speak with you, ma'am."

"Thank you, Tsubaki-san. I'll be heading to lunch after this phone call. You should too, so forward all calls to voice mail until after you get back."

"Hai. Yes, ma'am."

Sydni picked up the handset with a smile. "Hey chicklet, how are you?"

"Great! The designs are coming along wonderfully. And I've designed a little something for you, sis." It made Sydni feel good to hear the happiness stream through the phone. Charli was enjoying life, just like she'd always wanted her to.

One of the advantages of having a sister who

was a kick ass designer and tailor was that Sydni got to be the guinea pig for all the new designs. Well, it was usually a plus, unless Charli pulled something funky out of the hat like that orange velvet thing she'd tried to talk Sydni into wearing to a local charity fundraiser.

"So, what's up, Syd? You sound preoccupied. More so than usual, I mean."

"I, uh, I'm due to meet Drew for lunch any minute."

"You two have been thick as thieves. Dinner every night. Lunch every day. So, why don't you sound happier?"

"Same old concerns. Different day."

"Drew or work?"

"Take your pick. Look, I've got to run, so…"

"Oh no you don't, Syd. You're going to give me a clue before we get off this phone or I'm keeping the peach cobbler I made for you this afternoon."

"You made me peach cobbler?"

"Don't change the subject, woman. What's going on? I thought you and Drew were really hitting it off."

Sydni wiped her palm across her brow with a sigh. "Look, Charli, it's just that I don't know what to think or feel. The more time we spend together the more I wonder about…" A pause was required to get her head together. Besides, it was her fault that she hadn't brought these things up to Drew, and as far as he knew their relationship was just dandy. With a deep breath, she pushed on. "I don't doubt Drew's sincerity. And his love making skills? Dayum! I enjoy spending time with him. In fact, he's spoiled me for any other man. But what about years from now when the difference in our ages, let alone our races, begin to show?"

Sydni hit the speakerphone button, pushed back from her desk and started to pace in front of the huge window that overlooked the Expedex properties.

"Perhaps I'm being premature, Charli, but I haven't become successful by failing to plan or considering the results of my actions. What about ten or fifteen years from now? And what if the man wants children? By the time any child of ours reached age twenty, I'd be almost ready for social security while Drew was still in his prime. What then?"

"You mean other than the fact that you'll both be older," Charli quipped smartly.

Sydni ignored the remark and pushed on, letting all of her emotional baggage tumble to the carpet and fall open.

"God, there just seems to be such a huge gap between fifty-two and sixty. And sixty-two and seventy. Sheesh. Then there's our family and the herd of cows they'd have if I showed up in the South on Drew's arm."

"Why? Because he's white? Girlfriend, puh-lease," Charli chortled. Sydni wasn't sure what was so funny, but she was sure Charli would let it slip any second now. "Syd, you've never given a damn what anyone thinks, including our absent family. Hey, you know what just popped into my mind? Remember that guy I dated in high school? Mark Anthony?"

"Oooh, the hottie from Puerto Rico? Yes, how could I forget? He had a smile that made me want to drop to the floor and yell, do me now!" Sydni laughed, remembering the young man her sister had brought home for her to meet.

"And what about Peetie, from Guam? He was quite a looker too. And smart."

"True. Whatever happened to him, anyway?"

"Wait, wait," Charli said excitedly, "What about Ricky, with the deep dimples and stellar biceps? He went on to become a dentist. Didn't see that one coming."

Sydni paused. There was a method to her sister's madness, she was sure of it. "Charli, why are you bringing up people you haven't seen in fifteen years or more?"

"Because you never cared about the race of any man I ever brought home. So why…?"

"Okay, okay, I get it," Syndi said, throwing her hands up though her sister couldn't see through the phone. It didn't stop Charli from having her say.

"Look, sis, you took care of the both of us for years while the family you're suddenly so worried about went off to do their own thing. They left the state, Syd, leaving us to fend for ourselves. Why do you care what they think now? If Drew is what makes you happy, who are they to say you aren't entitled to him?"

Good point. In fact, Drew made her feel special, loved. Alive. And he appreciated her just the way she was, big ass and all. The man had no interest in constantly trying to change her into something or someone else. And loved to sex her up just the way she liked.

With a sigh she made her way back to the speakerphone. Pondering her sister's words, she said, "Thanks, sweet pea. Love you, Charli.

Gotta run."

"Love you too. Now go enjoy your lunch and stop tripping. You hear me, Sydni Lee?"

"Yeah, I hear you, Charli Marie. See you at dinner on Sunday evening?"

"Yep. Bye."

Speaking of Sundays, Drew even appreciated joining her in front of the television for a good football game. Even if he did like the Raiders. Well, nobody was perfect...but damn if Drew wasn't awful close.

Bottom line—could she get past the taboo of dating a younger man? A man she enjoyed both in and out of bed? Just the thought made her smile all the way to the Expedex restaurant-styled cafe.

Drew looked up and smiled, then stood and pulled out her chair. Gentleman to the bone. "Syd, you all right," he asked softly once he was seated.

Sydni could have kicked herself. She'd slipped back into thinking so hard and deep over the what-if's that she'd zoned right out.

God, Drew couldn't know what was on her mind. They'd already covered most of this ground in their endless talks—which she'd enjoyed, by the way—and surely the man was getting tired of her voicing the same tired concerns. This subject should be good and buried, yet it wasn't quite dead in Sydni's mind yet.

But before she could open her mouth to assure both him and herself, they were no longer alone.

"So, you're the new head of legal for Japan, eh?"

Interesting. Sydni had never noticed how pretty — young and pretty — Alexandra Voltier was. Until now.

Drew stood and extended his hand with a friendly smile. But there was no heat behind it. Nothing like the blinding, completely focused gaze he tended to pin her with.

"Yes. I was recently promoted into the Japanese division. I'm Drew. Drew Caruth." He shook her hand and sat right back down again.

"Mmm, yes, I know."

Was that a purr lacing Alex's words? Bitch. Sydni didn't make a sound, nor did she look up. Just stabbed the lettuce of her salad like she wanted to put a hole in the bowl. Drew looked her way but said nothing.

"So, Drew, how do you like working with Ms. Cannes in the Japan group? I hear she's a tough nut to crack, but once you get inside…she really knows her stuff." The woman didn't even bother to hide the real meaning of her words.

Sydni felt her lover's eyes on her but refused to look up or acknowledge the conversation.

"It's been awesome. The deals you all put together are a little different than what I'm used to, but everyone's been very helpful." Drew's words were laced with just the slightest, quickly hidden confusion.

"If there's anything I can do," the woman said with a sexy drawl that made Sydni's gaze finally snap up. "Anything at all, be sure and let me know."

Well, that was more than suggestive considering Alex's focus was on Drew's crotch while she handed him her card. With a big assed grin plastered across her face she said, "Perhaps lunch sometime. Or dinner? Or whatever." Hell, Sydni wondered when the woman's fangs would begin to show.

"Thank you for the offer," Drew returned smoothly. "But I usually have dinner with my woman."

God, she so couldn't deal with this right now. It was just too much, especially on the heels of all her insecurity. Not only were her thoughts in turmoil, but The Bitch chose that moment to poke her head into Drew's business. Well, maybe this was for the best. If Sydni gave him an out, opened a door for him to walk away from whatever it was they were developing, perhaps he'd take the opportunity to get with Alex? Take the chance to be with someone a bit closer to his own age.

Sydni stood so fast her chair shot back several inches and scraped the hardwood floor. Relieved that the thing hadn't crashed to the floor, she squared her shoulders and spoke evenly.

"I have some work to do. I'll catch you guys later."

Alex's smile quirked up into what could only be described as a predatory grin. "Perhaps I can keep Drew here company while he finishes his meal?"

"Be my guest," Sydni bit out, then snatched her plate off the table. She turned on her heel, biting her bottom lip to keep it from trembling as she dumped her uneaten food in the trash. All she gave Drew was a good view of her back as she retreated

Drew's expression remained schooled, but

his body language screamed "What the fuck?" But the instant surge of jealousy she felt, though unreasonable, had her inner witch peeking her head out to play. And not in a good way.

By the time she got to the elevator, her stomach boiled, skin flushed hotly, and temper flared. But Sydni was most angry at herself. Damn it, she'd never retreated in her life. That was something usually reserved for others to do to her, not receive from her. Yet, she'd bailed. With style, no doubt, but bailing was bailing no matter how classy it was done.

Too late. Sigh.

* * * * *

Drew appeared as a walking mountain of calm resolve. But just like the high peaks of a volcano he looked cool enough for snow to stick on the outside, while underneath the surface his anger boiled hot enough to melt rock. What the hell had Sydni been thinking practically throwing him to madam wolf, aka Alex Voltier? Oh just wait until he got his hands on that woman.

Even as a newcomer to the division, he'd already heard of this particular female. In fact, back in the days when he'd worked as an independent consultant on a few Expedex contracts, Alex's name has been floated past his ears as one of the hottest, yet coldest, females in the corporation.

So here he sat spending the remainder of his lunch time in Alex's office when he should be licking the inside of Sydni's sweet thighs for dessert. Damn women. Both of them.

Instead of sitting across her desk from him, Alex sank into the empty chair next to him, no doubt reserved for whoever would be on the receiving end of a royal tongue lashing. Crossing her legs, the undeniably sexy curve of her calf muscle brushed his knee. The light scent of perfume floated from her perfectly proportioned body. And none of it did a thing for him.

"So, Drew…"

Drew bit the inside of his lip to keep from curling it up in disgust. There was nothing he disliked more than a 'ho-style female who put herself out there for easy pickin'. Time to make it clear what his intentions were. And weren't.

A drawl that was probably supposed to come across as sexy dribbled past her lips. "Would you like to have this discussion over dinner? Or maybe breakfast." Alex re-crossed her legs, spreading her thighs more than was necessary before hooking her leg over her knee, swinging a high-heeled pump back and forth. Her smile was huge, but the frost behind her eyes was chilling.

"I'm flattered that a beautiful woman like you would give me such an invitation. But I'm seeing someone, Alex." Then he laid the stop-'em-in-their-tracks smile on her. Hmm. She didn't thaw. Not even a little.

Uncrossing her legs, she crossed them at the ankle and sat up a bit straighter in the comfy chair. A saucy tilt of her head was followed by another frosty grin.

"I understand, Drew. I'd heard you were single, and I'm single... Well, I hope you're not offended. You know, everyone suing everyone else these days."

"Suing? For what?"

"You know, sue me."

An uneasy slither worked its way into the individual bones of Drew's spine. What was going on here?

"For sexual harassment," Alex crooned with a pout. Too bad her contrition was lost by the hint of bitch behind her eyes.

He chuckled and waved her off, then scooted down comfortably in the chair as if he were at home watching the game. He hoped she bought his easygoing attitude because something whispered to him that the whole situation, as innocent as it appeared, was three kinds of wrong. "We're both adults here, Alexandra, so no worries."

"Alex, please."

"Sure, Alex. If complimenting someone or asking them to join you for a meal constitutes sexual harassment, then our society really needs help."

Of course that isn't what the wench had meant at all, but there was no way in hell Drew was going there. "But if you don't mind, I could really use some help. From what I hear you're the best person for this kind of stuff."

"Sure. What can I do for you?" Her expression brightened. Genuinely brightened. Interesting.

"I'm working the legalese for Ms. Cannes' division. And I'm trying to familiarize myself with how things are done. I know that after the contracts are signed for the division, they're sent to your department for expedition. I figured I'd start with the small electronics account with Sony. It seems straight forward enough to jump in with both feet, especially since it's already a done deal and I can't possibly screw it up by messing with the contract language."

The smile slid off her face and was replaced by a grim showing of teeth. Brrr. The chill was back along with...did the woman blanch? Drew could swear her skin color leached out of her face just now. Her expression was obviously glued on, but a flicker of concern reflected in those chipped emerald eyes of hers, he was sure of it.

"Sure. What questions can I answer for you?"

"Well, since you're the project manager for this account, can you help me understand the part of the contract that determines the payment schedule?"

She rose with a crisp, "Of course," then walked around the desk and sat down, pulling a cool curtain over her demeanor. So not good.

Chapter Nine

Fuming in her office a few hours later, Sydni tried to bury her head in some new contracts, a few mundane phone calls to clients and lots of dull paperwork. It wasn't working. Not even close.

With a hand at the small of her back, she slowly pressed into the tense muscles and rose from her desk. Standing at the floor to ceiling windows, she watched the sunset off in the distance, loving the purples and pinks reflected on the walls of her office. The automatic blinds began to close, slowly blocking out the first twinkling of stars in the clear twilight sky. Must be six o'clock.

In the middle of packing her briefcase and laptop her office door opened and closed with a sharp snap. Sydni didn't look up. No need. She'd recognize the heady scent of this particular visitor anywhere. Drew. She'd known it was him the second he walked in. Had actually expected him sooner. What had he and Alex been doing all this time? No, wait. Him doing Alex is what she wanted, wasn't it?

"Want to tell me what the hell that shit was about at lunch?"

A scowl, laid from one end of his brow to the other, accompanied the near snarl wrapped around his words. She pulled a deep breath into suddenly depleted lungs and sighed.

Did she want to try to explain? "No, not really."

"Too fuckin' bad, baby. I want to know what's going on in that beautiful, though no doubt misguided, brain of yours. Why did you bail on me and leave me with that…that woman?" He motioned furiously toward the door. His motions so sharp, even the sleeve of his exquisitely cut suit jacket snapped unhappily as he moved with irritated motions.

And the man was changing colors. If he got anymore pissed off he'd turn cherry-colored and blow a major gasket. In as soothing a voice as she could muster, Sydni spoke quietly and with conviction. Sort of.

"She's perfect for you, Drew. Alex is settled in her career, smart, beautiful, perky." There was that "P" word again. "And closer to your age."

"Damn it, Sydni, if I wanted someone my age I'd have them. And yes, I said them. Why the hell do we have to keep having this conversation?"

"Look, Drew, I really don't want to do this with you right now," she sighed with annoyance, her expression hard and determined to steer him clear of her. After she got rid of him, she'd dive into some work. That always took her mind off of things. Pitifully, it was all she really knew how to do, and do well. Relationships? Not so much.

"Well that's too damn bad because we're going home and we're going to deal with this. Then I plan to fuck you until you realize that I don't want anyone in my bed but you. Hell, I can't handle more than you."

"I have plans this evening. I'm not going home right now," she lied. Hell, all she'd done before meeting Drew was work, go home and work some more. Now after having him in her life, even for just a few weeks, the last thing she wanted was to totter around that big house alone...working.

"Then I guess I'll just have to follow you all over town until you end up at home. If I have to stay on your ass until you walk it through your door, Sydni, I have no problem with that."

Storm clouds remained in his wake after he yanked open her office door and carefully closed it behind him. Well, she could say this for the man—he had class enough to keep their argument private rather than slamming the heavy wood door and letting the whole division know.

Damn it, there must be something else to do other than drive around pretending to be out on the town. Maybe she'd straighten up her office? After a brief look around that idea lost appeal considering Tsubaki-san kept the place spic and span. Perhaps she'd have dinner out at that little jazz scene she enjoyed all too seldom? Sigh. No denying the fact that she simply didn't want to be in her own little one-some. She flipped her cell phone open, started to call Charli, then changed her mind. Sister or not, Charli would never understand what she'd been trying to do during that moment of—oh yes, she could admit it now—insanity when she'd pretty much abandoned Drew to the possibility of landing in Alex's arms.

Abandoned. God, that sounded so dramatic. Besides, pushing him toward Mizz Voltier had seemed like a perfectly great idea at the time. But after seeing the disappointment and indignant anger in Drew's beautiful grays, her grand idea now seemed plain old stupid.

Second guessing herself had never been a habit. But now it seemed as if every action, every idea, every thought was all wrapped up around a man she shouldn't want. The problem was the reasons she shouldn't want him were beginning to make less and less sense the more time they spent together.

Sydni took the elevator down to the second floor, then walked across the glass and steel skyway that connected Expedex to its private parking lot across the street. Row upon row of empty spaces left no doubt there was nobody else in the lot this late. The sound of her heels click-clicking against the pavement seemed to come from a million echo-filled miles away. Regardless of what Drew had said in her office, he'd obviously changed his mind about tailing her home. Could she blame him if he'd decided to say to hell with her and her emotional roller coasting? Wanting him one day, then tossing him at some other woman the next? Distracted, and practically running into one of the lampposts, Sydni made her way to her car. There was a hole in her stomach forty feet deep, and not from hunger, though she'd thrown away most of her lunch. What was she supposed to do now that she'd hurt Drew so deeply?

What a mess.

Briefcase tossed into the passenger seat of her car, Sydni climbed in, locked the door, fastened her seat belt and sat studying how the fluorescent lights shone over her car. On yet another forlorn sigh, her eyes slid closed and the marble-sculptured face of the man who had her tied up in knots appeared, then morphed from mad, to happy, to horny and back again. Suddenly her mind veered to the last time he'd slept over at her house. Wait, it had just been last night. Yet already her body missed him so much it felt like forever since he'd touched her, caressed and licked every inch of her skin. Just the thought of his talented hands working magic across her sensitive ass sent a warming pool of need to gather at the entrance to her suddenly glowing core.

The phone rang. Her heart jetted up into her throat.

"This is Sydni," she stammered, quickly masking her shock with a calm "you're bothering me" timbre—the one she used to use on Charli when she was younger. Didn't work worth a damn now, but it still sounded good and solid.

"Move it, Sydni. I only have so much

patience and you are pushing it, baby."

She looked up and there he was. He'd pulled his car right up to hers and she hadn't even noticed. No, you were too busy imagining his pole of a cock.

"Tantrums don't suit you, Drew," she blew out on a loud breath, then snapped the phone shut, amazed at how gorgeous the man was even when he was pissed off. Peeling out of her parking space, Sydni was glad he couldn't see her biting her lip trying not to chuckle.

And true to his word, the man stayed on her ass all the way to her house.

In fact, instead of parking on the street like he usually did, when the garage door went up Drew pulled inside, right into the empty space next to her. She cut the engine, let the door down and slowly got out of the car. Drew was there to take her hand and help her out.

He reached for the briefcase in her hand. It was a sweet gesture for him to carry her things inside. Allowing him to take the case from her suddenly nerveless fingers, she lowered her head. His words had her snapping it back up.

"You won't need this, Syd. No working tonight, except with me." Then he tossed the thing into the back seat, slammed the car door, and pulled her in his wake.

"Look, Drew, I'm not one for being manhandled, damn it. Let go of my hand, or slow the hell down."

He paused in the hallway leading from the garage door into the house, looked down at her feet and growled. The heat in his gaze flared, then ratcheted up a notch to flat out blazing.

"Damn, I'd forgotten you were wearing those fuck-me pumps. When I saw you put them on this morning I wanted to drag you back to bed and fuck you silly with nothing on but those sexy-as-hell shoes."

"What the hell does that have to do with what I just said?" She scowled for all she was worth, but his one-sided "I'm gonna wear you out" grin had her knees practically knocking together to keep her core from twitching. Damn man.

"As for manhandling, I don't believe it in." He leaned down and gently removed her shoes. "But tonight you're going to submit to me, Sydni."

On a step back, she said, "I don't do domination, thank you."

"You mean you *didn't* do domination. Tonight, you will."

He took her hand and they were once again flying through the house, straight to the bedroom.

"Drew, what the hell?"

"No talking."

"No talk...? What?"

This time he didn't answer, but stripped her where she stood until there was nothing between them but her goose-bumped skin. When he was done, the man simply pointed to the bed. And expected her to do it?

Puh. Right.

Sydni fixed her mouth to tell him to go to hell, but one glance at the thunderclouds roiling in his stormy gray eyes and she snapped her mouth shut instead. Her feet obviously had no qualms with obeying Drew considering they took off for the bed without a second thought, leaving her mind to stand there in front of him with a defiant glare. Not bothering to pull the covers back, Sydni climbed onto the bed and lay there shivering with anticipation. Knowing he would never harm her, her body hummed with excitement and wonder at what he would do next.

"Scoot to the middle, Syd, and close your

eyes."

With an indignant and completely non-heartfelt huff, she complied by rolling over twice and resting on her back, eyes closed, muttering under her breath. Eyebrows pulled down into a frown as she concentrated on the sounds around her. The slight squeak — she should really get that fixed — of the closet door opening answered some of her questions. But not all. What could Drew possibly be looking for amongst her clothes? A few moments later the bed shifted under his weight. Heat from his body told her he was very close. The breath against her cheek said he was closer than she'd first thought.

"No, don't open your eyes."

"Fine," she growled. Gorgeous bastard.

"Hands above your head."

Soft, wispy fabric sluiced over the flesh of her wrist and wrapped securely around it. Bare skin brushed against her forearm as he reached for the other hand. Something scalding hot and hard as metal thumped her shoulder. Oh-ho-ho! He'd obviously stripped while rummaging through her things 'cause Drew was now naked. His cock was a living flame and, from the swipe of moisture smeared on her shoulder, gloriously aroused.

Hmmm, what would that cock feel like nuzzled between her breasts while Drew pushed the mounds together and tugged on her nipples? Immediately the traitorous little nubbins stood at attention, drawn into tight little points. All from a thought?

A moment passed. There was no movement on the bed now but he was near. The heat from his skin enticed and tempted, just out of reach.

"Drew?" No answer. She called again. Still nothing.

In the deafening silence, Sydni's mind ran off on a tangent. It considered the wonderful possibility of things working out between her and Drew. What was stopping her from embracing this chance that destiny had brought to her doorstep anyway? After all, it wasn't everyday that a settled and seasoned man who was kind, possessed a keen mind, and looked fashion-magazine-quality gorgeous dropped into a woman's life…er, jail cell? Bed? Whatever.

She'd always taught her sister that it was not her responsibility to determine other people's choices. Was she doing the same to Drew? Trying to persuade him not to make a choice that he was well determined to make? Lord knows she wanted to be with him, so it wasn't like the attraction was one-sided. Sacrificing, or rather sabotaging, her own happiness to protect Drew from himself? Geez, what the hell kind of sense did that make?

Once again listening keenly to the sounds around her, a sliver of apprehension worked its way down the nerves of Sydni's spine. It was too quiet. Had Drew undressed her, then left her laying there like some half-trussed idiot? Maybe she should just forget this and get up now? A tug against the scarf on her wrists revealed she was going nowhere fast. The man had indeed tied her to the headboard in such a way that the scarves felt weightless unless she pulled against the bonds.

Her eyes flew open and her startled gaze crashed into Drew's determined one. Busted. He jerked his neck back and stared at her like she was out of her damn mind.

"Did I say you could open your eyes?" It was little more than a deep, very serious sounding whisper.

Not bothering to answer she slammed the lids shut. Now came uncertainty, followed by self-chastisement and a fair bit of guilt at being caught. On the other hand, she bit her lip to keep from chuckling at how girlishly silly it was to feel guilty at all.

"You've made this bed, Syd. Now lay in it."

And when a palm settled over the close cropped curls of her mound, Sydni's slick folds parted easily and welcomed his questing fingers. It couldn't be helped. The man just brought it out of her, and with so little effort it was downright disconcerting.

Yet, she had to make him see reason. Right? Had to make him see that...oh, god, see what? The little expedition traveling up and down the path between her legs was working her nerves, and so not in a bad way. Obviously, Drew was set on tipping the scales of reason in his favor.

"But..."

"Shush!"

"Oh hold the door. Did you just shush me, Drew Caruth?"

This time one hand played while the other landed over her mouth and stayed there. And without an ounce of remorse, either. Her mouth opened and closed a couple of times before a frustrated sigh left her lips. She'd just have to let her expression tell it all because she couldn't think of a single word.

"Yes, Syd, I said shush. What? You have something to say?" he challenged.

A groomed brow winged upward in question, but not another sound — harsh breathing didn't count — came forth.

"Close your eyes and keep them that way. Now woman, you will listen closely so I don't have to say this again."

He waited a moment until the tension leached from her shoulders and slid down to her thighs. Thighs that were beginning to quiver given the fact he played with her pussy. Stroking, parting, giving more than a woman could stand only to back off until she wanted nothing more than to beg him to continue.

"I need a woman who can handle me, Syd. Someone with a strong spirit who knows what she wants and won't be bowled over by an equally strong man. And that someone is Sydni Cannes. You. But for some reason you think I can't manage to remember how old you are, as if it matters or something."

As he spoke, those same gentle, but insistent fingertips teased her labia until they throbbed, ached, wanted. How as she supposed to listen when he was hell bent on plucking her strings like a newly strung banjo at somebody's southern ho-down? Good lord!

"If you let me, Syd, I can love you like no

one else. All I want is to give you everything I have, everything I am. Do you need me? No, but I'm glad you don't. The fact that you can and have taken care of both you and Charli only makes me want you more. And I always get what I want, baby. What do I have to do to convince you that you're the one, Sydni?"

Now came soft but firm pats just above her clit as two fingers slid into her juicy depths to add to the torment. Her stomach clenched, hips rolled as her body sought more of the exquisite sensation, needing her soul to ring with only the music he could create there.

Then his mouth was in motion, molding itself to the very shape of her sex, lapping the tender folds. When his fingers slid out, his tongue dipped low to feast on the nectar creaming his face. His fingers slid in and that tongue wrapped around her clit, tugging, sucking. In...suck. Out...lick. God, it was too much.

Orgasm number one began as a tingle just below the crease where ass met thigh, then circled around to her core. Sweat soaked the comforter beneath her. Even the back of her knees were slick with moisture. A scream gathered at her toes, traveled up her trembling body and blasted out of her mouth as she came long and hard, until her head flew from side to side in entreaty. It was too much, yet not enough.

"Oh god! Drew!"

But Drew didn't answer, nor was he finished. Instead of answering her call, he pushed her into the next release. The thing circled 'round and 'round her womb, building until it exploded and surged through every nerve, every cell, turning her into nothing more than a panting mass of acquiescence.

Drew hummed his pleasure into her soaked flesh and all she could think of was, yes, yes, and more yes. The vibration between her legs ceased as he lifted his head.

"Look at me, Syd."

Garnering her strength for whatever would be reflected in his beautiful eyes, Sydni eased her lids open, lifting her head just enough to meet his gaze between her thighs. Her lips parted on a swift intake of air. Raw longing, deep aching need, and vulnerability all shone there, taking her breath away at the swirl of emotion emanating from his gaze. Honeyed nectar, her nectar, covered his chin. The talented pink organ that had just driven her to the stars left an even wetter path across his already wet lips.

"Say you want me too, Syd. Tell me, baby."

Crawling half way up her body before sitting back on his knees, the tension in the air was palpable as Drew reigned in every swirling emotion and stark craving. He went stone still and waited. Waited to know what she wanted. Willing to stop if what she wanted wasn't him.

Sydni's resolved splintered and fell away even as she tried to push one last button.

"But what about kids, Drew? Surely you want kids? And I'm just not feeling that at this time in my life. And what about my family? Mine are so countrified and not necessarily up with the times of interracial relationships."

"Listen darlin'," he drawled in his best down home country imitation. "I. Want. You. And I'll take whatever I can get. Even if I had everything I wanted in life, you'd still be an upgrade to me, woman. Besides, I'm sure Charli will have plenty of kids for us to spoil. Then after Aunt Syd and Uncle Drew are done spoiling them we can send them home to their parents and have the house to ourselves. I'm already dreaming about showering Charli's future babies with love. Hell, I'm dying to give you some rug burn fucking in front of the fireplace, after busting my ass on one of the grandbaby's toys sitting in the middle of the floor. As for your family, last I heard it wasn't your style to let anyone, even them, make decisions for you. Unless you're not up to the challenge." he teased lovingly.

The man was too much.

Knowing that Drew envisioned their relationship as gaining the world rather than throwing away his future, Sydni felt all kinds of special. This man saw her as a serious asset to his life, someone who brought him balance, would give him a challenge, and allow him to fulfill her needs, all rolled into one warm, giving, horny little ball of a woman.

"So, what'll it be, Syd. You and me? Think carefully because I am prepared to pursue you to no end, baby."

Unable to form the words, all Sydni could do was nod her head and swallow down the emotion gathered in her throat.

"Aw, baby, you've made me the happiest man on the planet." And just like that, he set to work. "God, I just want to brand you, write my name all over that succulent pussy of yours. Hell, climb up into your soul until I can't tell where you begin and I end."

Sydni laughed, cried and sighed as his tongue left a warm trail along her collarbone while strong fingers gently tugged at a puckered nipple.

What an idiot she'd been. She'd claimed to have been looking at things from what was supposedly Drew's position. But what she'd really been doing was hiding behind her own fears. Fears that she couldn't really find or hold a man who was comfortable with who she was. Who didn't care she was a big executive at an international corporation. A man who was so solid in his own skin, he wasn't intimidated by the natural strength of character that made up Sydni Cannes. All that insecurity had been hidden, blanketed by diving into her work, trying to ignore the loneliness shadowing her steps every day simply because her previous lovers, instead of accepting her, had tried needlessly to compete with both her career and the love for her sister.

Still on his knees, Drew lifted Sydni's hips and settled her slick pussy just over the flared head of his cock. Poised at her entrance Sydni held her breath as gentle strokes lit up the skin from her ass clear up to the back of her knees. Legs fell open when Drew set his cock in motion, stretching her hole as he pushed forward. Sydni felt her entire bloodstream flow to the spot just above her creaming gate, making her clit throb.

Drew's voice dropped to a sexy growl.

"I'm man enough to go after what I want. And I want you." Running his hands over her thighs, over her stomach and up to her full breasts, he said, "No stick figure, barely old enough to drive women for me, Syd. I'd break them, inside and out. Not on purpose, of course, but I'm a driven man, and not always easy to deal with. I'd just run right over them. Plus, I tend to demand good hard fucks from my lovers. Not to mention I seem to have this knack for being stubborn, perfect, always right..."

A snort burst out of her chest before she could stop it. Always right indeed? Then the tip of his dick slipped in an inch, just past the ring of muscle at the door of her channel. Her body instinctively clamped down on it, trying to hold the wide tool inside. Her snort faded on a frustrated sigh when he withdrew.

Short shallow digs stoked the smoldering flames licking her skin until her breath whooshed through her lungs trying to catch up to the pleasure streaking through her nervous system. In. Out. In. Out. Not nearly enough to sate, but just enough to make her reach out for him. She was eager to play in the silky slide of the soft locks on his head, fingers buried to the scalp. Then down to the short downy hair on his perfectly sculpted chest. The dips and hollows of abs so well-defined she could snowboard across them. But her wrists were securely attached to the slats of the bed's headboard. Damn it.

If he didn't fuck her, really fuck her soon she would simply go up in smoke and Charli could scatter her ashes out over the lake. Perhaps she should have written a last will and testament before pushing Drew to such a possessive state that he felt compelled to prove she was the one for him?

"Beg for it. Tell me you want it, that you want me."

"Oh god, yes. I want it, want you. Please, Drew." A full, deep slide parted the sleek inner muscles clear to the entrance of her womb causing a gasp at the fullness. And back out again until the fat head nudged her entrance again. And then he stopped. Shit!

"No more shoving me at other women, Syd?" A firm thumb drew circles over her clit with ever increasing speed.

"No, no more shoving," she ground out,

lifting her hips urgently for want of a different kind of shoving. "Drew. Oh god, I promise. Please."

Drew drove home in one stroke. And this time he hung around for awhile.

* * * * *

Oh she could really get used to waking up like this. Drew's arms surrounded her with the kind of warmth only possible from skin-on-skin contact. And he currently filled her with the kind of steel 'n silky hardness only he could give her. And that hardness happened to be slowly sliding between her thighs, rubbing up against her clit from behind.

In no time she thoroughly creamed the steely hardness rubbing against her, instantly greedy to be filled again.

"Good morning," he sighed against her nape. "How 'bout some Saturday morning dick for that sweet pussy of yours?"

Oh dear god, yes. Her sensitive flesh twinged from the delicious reaming it had received last night, but the damn thing just couldn't seem to get enough. Guess greedy was an understatement.

Reaching back, Sydni sank her fingers into the soft hair on Drew's head and pulled him to her shoulder. Immediately his tongue came out to play with the sweet spot that made her squirm. Oh yes, right there where shoulder and neck muscles twined together.

Instantly soaking wet Sydni was consumed with need for Drew to satisfy her. And not just physically, but somehow he'd managed to sink into the very depths of her soul and take up residence there. And it only made her body react to him all the stronger.

Drew lifted her leg and pushed with his hips. The second Sydni's nervous system registered the delicious stretch and burn of that fabulous cock, it went into overdrive.

"God, that's so good," she moaned, pushed her ass back at him as he slid deeper. Suddenly her whole being stood on the brink of falling apart. "Fuck me, Drew."

"I know you're sore, Syd. Let's take it easy." His strokes remained even as he made gentle love to her.

She lifted her leg, reached back and stroked the base of his rod as it moved gently in and out of her.

"Oh god, please. I'm on fire. I need it."

"Mmmm, are you sure, sweet? I don't want to hurt you."

"Hurt me, damn it!" Her hips swiveled and she tightened the muscles of her pussy knowing he couldn't resist the extra pressure applied to his already engorged cock.

"Damn, Syd, you're wicked."

"Damn right. Now harder."

The speed of his thrusts increased, along with her heart rate. His breath cooled the sweat filming the back of her neck. Right on that spot.

"Bite me there," she pleaded. He did. She lost it.

With a wild shriek, Sydni yanked the covers off their writhing bodies, pushed up off the firm mattress and leveraged herself until she was on top and still impaled on Drew's lovely cock. With her back to him, feet planted on the bed, she squatted and bounced like a cowgirl at a rodeo.

Yee haw!

Drew's fingers dug into the cheeks of her ass, putting his hips in motion and adding to the madness. He lifted her. Let her drop as his cock surged deep.

"Oh shit! Yes," she growled. "That's it, baby. Give it to me."

Hard, fast. Now. Exactly what she needed.

They fell apart together, each calling out the

other's name.

When they could breathe again, Drew urged her out of bed and to the shower. To her surprise, he bundled her in her favorite bath robe and led her downstairs to the family room where he made her sit while he made breakfast. To Sydni's surprise, he'd gotten Charli to give up her favorite recipe — apple upside down pancakes.

After a delicious breakfast, they sprawled in a tangle of arms and legs on the couch enjoying easy conversation.

"What are you doing next week and the week after?"

"Work. Why?" Sydni answered on a lazy yawn.

"I'd like you to come on vacation with me."

Vacation? When was the last time she'd taken one of those? It wasn't from a lack of desire to take time off. It simply wasn't that appealing to go alone. Charli often invited her to take off on trips with her friends who happened to almost always be male. Third-wheeling simply wasn't Sydni's style.

"You just started a new position with the company. How can you afford to take vacation time right now?"

"Part of my signing bonus. They needed me in the position just as much as I wanted to accept it. I already had vacation planned, so the powers that be had no problem with me negotiating to keep it, rather than push it off until later. So, you game? All you have to do is say yes and pack. I'll take care of all the little details."

It was awfully tempting. But there was the anomaly on the invoices against the Sony purchase order that needed looking into, though nobody seemed concerned about it except her.

But Drew was kissing her again, wiping away what little resistance she thought she had. Sydni heard herself agreeing to go to New Zealand. And by the time Drew was finished laying it down on her, she would have agreed to anything.

Chapter Ten

Alfred Pawn rolled over in the big bed and stretched awake. Every muscle between neck and knees was deliciously sore from the romp he'd shared with Viktor this evening. But where was his lover? The cooling sheets indicated he couldn't have been out of bed long. Perhaps he'd just gone to the bathroom?

Alfred lay back on the pillows with a sated sigh, stroking his limp cock in memory of all that Viktor had done to the semi-sore member. Mmm. God, what a wonderful lover. A twinge of guilt settled in his gut for a second when thoughts of Alex Voltier intruded. Alfred tried to remember why he was cheating on Viktor with Alex in the first place.

Alex had promised him a cut of the two million dollars they stood to gain from a bit of creative book keeping. That, in addition to being Alex's exclusive lover, had convinced Alfred to walk a thin line with Viktor, who'd been nothing but kind to him, though a bit demanding in the bedroom. Alex, on the other hand was a marvelous fuck with a wicked streak a mile long.

What drew him to her? The excitement of cheating, perhaps? Or the long-buried freak that the woman tended to bring out in him?

What he shared with Viktor was mutually warm and exclusive. But with Alex it was flat out explosive.

Alfred hoped his lover never found out. The last thing he wanted was to hurt Viktor, but Alex drove a hard bargain and an even harder riding crop. Alfred couldn't decide who wielded the thing better, Alex or Viktor. But one thing was for sure—if Viktor ever found out Alfred was having an affair, and with a woman of all creatures, there would be the devil to pay.

A muffled, barely audible shriek had Alfred scrambling from the big bed, heart slamming into his throat with alarm. What the hell was that? Shit! There it was again. The sound was urgent.

And where the hell was Viktor?

Creeping from the bedroom on bare feet, Alfred started to ease into his clothes, but a whisper of self-preservation told him to leave them. The last thing he needed was for his clothes to rustle if he came upon a burglar. Out of the door and down the hall, he came up on a room he hadn't noticed before. Actually, in the months he'd been with Viktor they seldom made it past the bedroom. A flush worked its way up his neck and into his cheeks as his cock began to stir with the thought of making love with Viktor. A scream sent the blood rushing away from his dissipating erection and straight to his heart.

Pressing his ear to the door he heard a distinctly male voice. But that voice hadn't made such a strangled urgent sound.

He turned the knob slowly and released a pent up breath when it slid open without a sound, cracked just enough to get a peek inside. Alfred's blood ran cold.

A buck naked Alex Voltier's hands were tied to what looked like a padded sawhorse. Bent over, legs spread wide, back at a perfect ninety-degree angle. A little green vibrator hummed in her pussy.

And Viktor's talented cock shuttled in and out of Alex's ass.

The woman begged, screamed almost incoherently when what must have been a cataclysmic orgasm ripped through her. Her thighs visibly trembled until Alfred was sure she would have buckled to the floor without the padded table holding her up. And Viktor kept right on fucking the hell out of her.

"These walls are soundproofed but if you don't stop screaming I'll have to gag you. I can't have you accidentally disturbing the guest in my bed."

"He sleeps like the dead," Alex panted. "I can't help screaming. It hurts so good."

"Yes, well, let's finish this shall we. I must get back to him before he wakes." After a particularly wicked stroke, Viktor moaned, "Mmm, the pawn's ass is almost as delicious as yours."

The pawn?

Alfred's gut churned. God, he was going to throw up.

Viktor's voice reached out into the room again. "I'm waiting, Alex."

Alex sucked in a breath and rasped, "I won't question. I will do as I am told. And only come when allowed."

"Again," Viktor demanded, stuffing himself into her passage.

Alfred's gut clenched at the sound of Alex gasping out a deep breath. She rambled between each stroke of Viktor slamming into her flesh. "I won't question. I will do as I am told. And only come when allowed."

Viktor and Alex? Pawn? Son of a bitch.

Chapter Eleven

"Blanket, sir?" the too-friendly stewardess asked, while practically rubbing her perky-assed tits all over Drew's shoulder. He looked up at her with a deep frown marring his brow. He took that moment to reach back, loop his arm around Sydni's shoulders and practically hauled her into his lap.

"No, thanks. I brought my own. Can't have my babe underneath something that probably hasn't been washed in a year."

Sydni wasn't sure whether to chuckle at his snarky comment or cringe at the thought of handling the airline blanket. "You can get me a soda, though. Something brown with caffeine. And a cranberry juice for my sweetie here."

She bit her lip when Drew tilted his head in her direction. Man, if the stewardess could have tossed 'em both off the plane at thirty-seven thousand feet with a look, she and Drew would be growing wings and learning how to fly about ten seconds ago.

Perky Boob Woman flounced away.

"You are a really bad boy, you know that?" Sydni whispered on a barely suppressed giggle-sigh.

He'd pulled a comfy fleece blanket out of a bag he'd toed underneath the seat in front of him, draped it over both their chilled bodies, and was in the middle of doing all kinds of wicked things to her thighs with his fingers.

"I'm only bad with you, beautiful. Now..." he breathed in her ear. "Spread those sweet thighs for me just a bit."

"I can't spread my legs on a commercial flight," Sydni hissed. Drew's audacity was second to none. But since it was all her fault the man stayed in a constant state of horny-ness, she certainly wasn't going to complain.

"Nobody can see with the blanket over us. And there's a lot to be said for flying first class. Lots of leg room."

His palm landed in her lap and nudged. When she wouldn't part them, he eased his fingers to a certain place on her knee and pressed. She was ticklish there and her legs flew open all on their own.

"Drew, stop it," she warned, cheeks heating rapidly. God, the man had everything blushing, the cheeks on her face, the cheeks of her ass and the soon-to-be pouty lips of her sex.

His hand eased back and forth across her skin. Why in the world had she decided to wear a damn skirt on the plane anyway. His eyes were locked with hers, but his expression had taken on a somewhat dreamy, distant look.

"Drew?"

"Look, woman, I have to get my fix," he said seriously, trying to look all kinds of innocent. Didn't work. Perhaps it was due to the devilish grin that he tried to keep from spreading across his lips. "I'll never make it the next twelve hours without touching you."

"Well, I'll never make it if you do touch me."

"Sure you can. Just cum quietly."

Dear god, what had she done to deserve this? Whatever it was, it had obviously been something really, really good. Or really, really bad.

Drew's lips approached one of the many sensitive spots on her neck that he'd found since they'd become lovers. This one was just below her left ear. The pads of two fingers had just tapped her rapidly swelling clit when the flight attendant returned, practically thrusting Drew's Coke into his face.

Drew ignored the woman with practiced

ease. Without missing a single nip or tug on Sydni's earlobe, he said in as deadpan a voice she'd ever heard, "Oh. You're back. Just sit the drinks down and there'll be nothing else. At least not right now. Later we may need a warm towel."

And he proceeded to lick a path up Sydni's neck so blatantly hot it wrung a gasp and a shudder from Sydni. The man didn't bother to acknowledge how wide the other woman's eyes became, nor how much they narrowed before she departed.

* * * * *

So far vacationing with Drew had been a blast. Sydni was having an awesome time exploring the land of The Lord of the Rings. There couldn't possibly be another place like New Zealand anywhere on Earth. And certainly not another man anywhere like Drew. In addition to arranging the most out-of-the-way accommodations, he'd arranged helicopter tours of some of the locations where the movie had been filmed. The land was wild and untamed in places, bringing to mind certain scenes from her favorite epic film. And she had her own action hero in a rugby player's body, but with a more stylish haircut.

Sydni leaned back in her chaise and frowned down at the baby powder fine sand underneath her feet, debating whether she wanted to swim and get sand up her ass, or just lay here and watch Drew play. Raising her gaze, she watched her man approach and had to force herself to breathe. As usual.

Rising up out of the waves, Drew dripped sex. After planting his surf board into the sand every step he made toward her sent her stomach rippling up into her throat. The water dripped down his body in sparkling rivulets, leaving wet paths in the downy hair of his bare chest. Packed slabs of muscle bunched and flexed as he wicked the water down and away from his arms. God the man had the most delicious thighs and well-formed calves she'd ever seen on a man. And an ass to simply die for, which happened to be nicely outlined by his soaked swim trunks.

His dark mop of hair was plastered to his head, curling about the ends as he made his way toward her, dripping wet. The dripping made her think of how he made other things...drip.

Yes, he looked great in shorts, and even better in nothing. His chaise groaned as he settled down in it right next to her with a contented sigh.

"Whoever thought sex on the beach was a great idea must have been crazy," Sydni mumbled watching him try to get the stuff off his legs. It hung on to the fine little hairs for dear life.

"Not crazy, just a fraud."

"You mean the person who thought of selling it as something sexy had never done it before?"

"Exactly. Who would be stupid enough to fuck on the beach? The last thing a man wants is sand up his cock."

Sydni laughed, enjoying Drew's wit. She settled deeper into the cushions of her lounger, more relaxed than she'd been in years. In truth, the man made her feel comfortable. Like an old robe or her favorite pair of slippers, she was becoming so used to his presence, she didn't want to think of what it would be like without him. Nor did she want to think about breaking in a new pair of comfies.

Sigh. Yes, Drew was a keeper.

After a few minutes of trying to read her novel, her attention was caught by a movement from the direction she couldn't keep her eyes from straying to anyway. Drew had risen and now stood next to her. She looked up and came face to face with a cock pushing against the front of his swim shorts. Oh boy.

Sydni dropped her book, grasped his hand and let him lead her into the house and straight to the shower.

After rinsing the sand from their bodies, Drew snatched Sydni's favorite massage oil off the dresser and headed for the screened-in private veranda out back.

"Coming?" he tossed over his shoulder. She grabbed a couple of clean towers and scrambled after him. Naked, he lay down on the leveled lounge and held out the bottle to her. "Do me, first?"

No problems there. Touching the man, easing her fingers over those miles of muscles, teasing him with her hands until he went crazy. Yep, she could certainly do him first.

She took the bottle from his hands and dumped a liberal amount into her palm, rubbing it back and forth so the friction would warm it. Working her fingers into the muscles of his shoulders and upper back she massaged and stroked, smiling at his groan of appreciation.

"God, that feels so good, Syd." After a few sighs and moans she eased up on that part of his back and concentrated on the tight muscles around his lower spine. Then it was down to his perfectly formed, trophy-deserving backside. Pressing her elbow into the hollow of one butt cheek she applied pressure a bit at a time to loosen the muscle. It was amazing how much stress a person carried in their butt cheeks. And since she planned to make sure Drew worked his thoroughly later, it was only fair to make sure he was good and relaxed now.

Working her way down his hamstrings, she finished with his calves and finally his feet. And since she'd been wicked, pressing hot open mouthed kisses and little nips to his heated skin from the time she started the massage, she wasn't surprised to find a fully erect cock rising up to greet her after she instructed him to turn over.

"You are a wicked, wicked woman." She grinned until he said, "And payback is a bitch." He flashed a lascivious grin as he sat up, swung his legs off the low lounge and stalked her. "Your turn."

Sydni took off at a dead run.

There was one thing he'd learned about Syd on this trip—the woman could run for the U.S. Olympic team if she'd been so inclined. Quick as a whip and agile, his sweetheart had a pair of legs that weren't just for show.

But today, he was ready for her. The second she took off out of the veranda and around the side of the house, he was on her in a flash. Shrieks, followed by wild giggles, filled the private alley when his arm snaked around her waist and hauled her back against his chest.

"Little minx," he murmured against her ear, then proceeded to tickle her until she squealed. All the while the crease of her glorious backside tortured his cock as she tried to get away.

Drew's tickling morphed into sensuous slides of his fingers over bare skin. Her giggles became sighs as her back rubbed against sensitive male nipples. She sucked in a ragged breath as one of his hands slid over her belly and up to palm a warm breast. The other lowered to tease the pouty lips of her now glistening sex.

So that little massage back there turned you on as much as it did me?" he whispered into her ear before pulling the lobe into his mouth to suckle.

"Oh god, yes," she panted. The swivel of her hips and arch of her lovely back screamed how far gone she was. God, the woman was so hot and uninhibited something inside of Drew snapped. He had to have her now.

Drew's fingers slid through the folds of her labia. As always she was amazed at how the easy glide of those fingers were so at odds with the brute strength that lay just underneath the surface. So tender, yet so strong. Sensitive, but as far from sappy as East was from West. Dominant, caring and giving. How on earth did the man find room in that body of his for all the different facets that made him who he was?

"God, Syd, you're so wet for me."

Suddenly, Sydni found herself whirled around and pressed up against the nearest surface — a wall on one side of their carport.

"I can't wait, Syd. I need you now."

And in one stroke, he was home. Balls deep in her cocoa pink heat, the flared head of Drew's cock stroked over bundles of nerve endings, making her shiver. She'd already been hot after giving him her little teasing rub down. Now her pussy was a-blaze and she needed relief right damn now.

With one leg pulled up over the crook of his elbow, Sydni held onto Drew's biceps for balance as he pushed into her like a madman. Fast, deep, hard strokes that sent her streaking toward climax so fast her head spun dizzily.

"Is it good, baby?" he panted.

"Yes. God, yes," she yelled, trying to move her hips to meet his strokes. It was so good. Hell, beyond good. Sydni wasn't sure there was a word for the explosive attraction they shared.

"Fuck!" Drew growled, trying to get even deeper. The muscles in his neck began to strain and stand out in stark relief to the smooth planes of his chest. He was wound up tight. And Syd wanted him to blow right along with her.

Sydni felt her climax gathering power as it circled around and around her womb. Then Drew reached behind her, dipped his finger in the dewy cream where his cock disappeared into her pussy, then smeared it around her puckered rear hole. The sensation sent her rocketing toward the edge.

Then he slipped the tip of a finger inside. Sydni toppled over that edge. But Drew didn't go with her. The man had something altogether different in mind.

Plucking Sydni completely off her feet, Drew hurried back through the house and out the backdoor to their private stretch of beach, still buried deep in Sydni's lush, warm body.

He stopped in front of the lounger where it

all began.

Sydni looked down and laughed, squeezing his cock, making him groan.

"You know good and well this little ole beach lounge is not going to hold our heavy asses."

"Of course not," he leered. "I plan to hold your ass, while the chair holds mine."

He sat down, careful to keep her sweet pussy wrapped around his gridiron cock. Straddling him, her feet were planted firmly in the sand. The angle was just the slightest bit different and made the ride nothing short of exquisite.

"Ride me, baby. Take me hard," he entreated, eyes almost crossed with lust. And she did. Rode him hard and wild, just like he wanted.

"Oh this is so…so…" Yeah, he knew exactly how she felt. He couldn't seem to find the words either.

Sydni was positive she'd never been so full of cock before. This position was different than riding from her knees. Her feet in the sand gave her just a bit more leverage, caused her hips to cant just a bit more forward. In turn Drew's cock stroked a bundle of nerves that had never experienced the touch of a man's flesh. Eyes closed, Sydni let the sensations wash through her—the oneness she felt with her lover, the soft scented ocean breeze blowing across her bare skin, softness of the powder-fine sand sifting through her toes. The fine short hairs of Drew's groin rubbing against her tender folds. His fingers plumping her nipples as he made a space for himself inside her body.

The last rays of the sun shone on her back as it seemed to slide into the sea. And the voice of the man she couldn't imagine being without told her, for the first time, that he loved her.

Chapter Twelve

After spending a couple of days recuperating from jet lag, it was time to go back to the office. And once Sydni got there, she wished she'd stayed in bed when Tsubaki-san patched a call through from one of the secretaries upstairs.

Sydni listened carefully unable to keep her mouth from falling open in shock. This couldn't be right. No way. No how.

"What the hell are you talking about?" Sydni demanded from the woman on the phone.

The secretary hissed in response, obviously trying to keep her voice down. "I said…"

"I know what you said. Now what the hell did you really mean?" Sydni didn't think she'd been this upset since the day her parents announced they were moving back to the South just as Charli was due to start her first semester of college.

Unfortunately, they'd taken their money with them and Sydni had to figure out how to pay for Charli's books and get her tuition in so she could actually start classes on time. And she'd had no million dollar bonuses headed her way from anywhere at the time.

"Drew Caruth was just led out of the building by security. He'd just come into his office a half-hour before and booted up his laptop when the senior management team called him up here. Next thing I knew, security showed up and took him out. They didn't even let him go back to his desk to get any of his personal things. I heard him ask someone to at least have his administrative assistant bring his briefcase and keys so he could get into his car. Rumor has it that Alex Voltier is behind this. Claiming sexual harassment or some such."

"Son of a bitch!" Sydni didn't even bother hanging up the phone and was out her door in a flash. When she got to Drew's office his things appeared undisturbed. Good. She'd gotten there before anyone else had a chance to ransack his belongings. Sydni packed his stuff as quickly as possible.

She knew it was a risk, but one she had to take. There was no way in hell Drew had committed such a crime. But if there was anything that might clear him, it was probably somewhere in this room.

Her hand was on the top of his laptop,

lowering it so it would shut down so she could toss it into his big attaché case with everything else that looked important.

Whoa, what was this? Just as she was closing the laptop, an instant message alert flashed at the bottom of his screen. Curiosity got the better of her.

I hope I don't end up like that cat who did the whole curiosity thing, she thought, then clicked on the little icon noting the date was the same day they'd left for vacation. Obviously Drew hadn't had a chance to check his messages.

'Hey handsome. I'm glad you weren't upset at our little interaction. Hope I answered all of your questions. And most of all, thank you for being a gentleman. Good luck with everything. And let me know if you change your mind about dinner…or any other things you might happen to want. Always, Alex.'

Hmm. What was that about?

Sydni closed the IM, careful to save it first, then reached for the files that were open on his desk. One of them was the Sony contract. The same damn one that had her stumped before. Drew had highlighted several sections with questions and comments. Looked like he was on to something. But Sydni didn't have time to figure it out now. She had to get out of here before anyone caught her. If the Expedex security folks got here before she could get out again, they'd confiscate everything. They certainly wouldn't give him his laptop. No, they'd scrub it clean and send it back to inventory. They'd also probably overlook the little note from Alex that might be all it took to get Drew off the hook in the first place.

The only things she left were his keys on the desk and his suit jacket on the hook behind the door. Silently locking up behind herself, Sydni put the thick leather strap over her shoulder and hauled Drew's attaché to her car then returned to her office for a second.

After placing a few bogus off-site meetings on her calendar she intercommed her secretary.

"Tsubaki-san, I'm heading out for some last minute meetings. I'll be back right after lunch. With that she made a call to Charli on her way out of the parking lot.

Drew couldn't believe it. The one woman he'd made crystal clear that he wasn't interested in sex was now claiming he'd harassed her for sex. He wondered when the hell that was supposed to have happened considering he and

Sydni had been out of the country for the past two and a half weeks. Bitch.

Well, at least they didn't take my phone, he mused as he clicked it open. It was Charli's phone number.

"Hey, Charli."

"Hey, you," Charli responded. "Where are you?"

"I'm on the way home. Security just brought me my keys and my suitcoat."

"Good. I'm on my way to your house," she paused. "With your things."

"Really? Great. See you shortly and thanks."

He knew Sydni was responsible and floored the gas, moving as quickly as he was able toward his destination.

Chapter Thirteen

It had been two weeks since Drew had been suspended from his position. He'd spent his days piecing together whatever he was onto in regard to the electronics shipping deal that had him stumped before. And Sydni got more and more pissed off the longer he dug into it. He'd said it involved Alex Voltier, but the stubborn man wouldn't tell her what it was, saying he didn't want her involved in case it all went to hell in a hand basket. So she'd quietly allowed him to borrow her copies of the contracts and let him do his lawyer thing.

She'd managed to use her standing in the company to get the senior partners who served on the board of directors to hear his defense instead of taking it to arbitration, or worse, to the District Attorney. Sydni sat in her chair feeling more like bacteria under a microscope than a senior executive at this firm.

"It is exactly eight a.m., Ms. Cannes. Let's begin." This from Mr. Epps, a literal senior partner. The man was so old, Sydni was sure he'd invented dirt. He was a no nonsense kind of man, but he was also fair. Just as she opened her mouth to address the board Drew chose that moment to enter the room.

"Excuse me, sir, I apologize for being late. May I?" he asked motioning to a seat across the conference room table from Sydni.

She took a deep breath and put her cards on the table. "Mr. Epps, members of the board, I don't believe Mr. Caruth harassed Alexandra Voltier."

"And why is that, Ms. Cannes," Mr. Epps asked in a bored, or perhaps tired, voice.

"Because, sir, we've been dating since before he received the promotion to my division. He's spent practically every hour he hasn't been working, with me."

"Really? You know how we feel about nepotism here, Ms. Cannes."

Drew cleared his throat.

"Excuse me," he said. Every head swiveled his way and paid him their utmost attention. Clearly the man was wearing his lawyer hat. He addressed the board with a simple, "If I may?" while motioning toward the front of the room.

With a nod of the senior partner's head, he stood and addressed the board.

"Ladies and gentlemen of the board,

nepotism can't be used against Ms. Cannes in this case. I came to work here without her knowledge, and had accepted the job offer before we'd ever met. She also had no knowledge of my promotion into her division. Also, we'd have to be related by blood or marriage in order for nepotism to be a factor. And neither of those circumstances exists. Though I hope to rectify the situation soon."

His gaze found hers as he flashed a smile, then turned away. Sydni's mouth fell so wide open she was sure she tasted the fuzz on the carpet beneath her shoes. Oh my god. The man was simply too bold. And he hoped to rectify the fact that they weren't related? By marriage?

The ancient skin of the senior associate's face almost cracked with his wide smile. "No wonder you're on the legal team, young man. Well said, and it gets Ms. Cannes off the hook. However, it doesn't quite do the same for you."

"Again, if I may, sir?"

"Why the hell not? You seem to be on a roll." This brought a chuckle from a couple of the other stern-faced board members. Others remained grim, reminding Sydni of how serious this matter was.

"Thank you, sir," Drew said. There went the

twinkle in his eye that she was becoming more and more familiar with. What was he up to?

"Ms. Cannes and I have been working to get me caught up on the Japan accounts. While she is the Executive Vice President of International Shipping, it is not her responsibility to oversee each and every customer account. Do you agree, sir?"

"Of course. We have hundreds of customers. There is no way a single person could oversee them all. What's your point?"

"Well, it is the project managers assigned to each account who actually oversee the day-to-day activity with our customers in regard to expedition of the agreements and fulfillment of contractual obligations. Yet, because Ms. Cannes is one of the few who does get involved with each of her division's customers she noticed something irregular with a recent account that she personally landed for one of our larger client's electronics division."

"Oh?" asked Mr. Epps.

All eyes pinned Sydni to her chair. While confident in her ability to skin and grin with the best of 'em she didn't enjoy so many eyes scrutinizing her just now. She almost sighed with relief when Drew continued and every gaze swung his way.

"After learning my way around how you all do things here, I went back and looked over the deal, keeping in mind the irregularities that Ms. Cannes had been trying to rectify. She'd even had several talks with the project manager and the accountant handling things on our end."

"And?"

"Independently, and without Ms. Cannes knowledge, I also spoke to the project manager, Alex Voltier, a couple of days before Ms. Cannes and I went on vacation together to New Zealand. Notice," Drew said as he passed around a screenshot of his IM from Alex. "Notice the date on the message to me from Ms. Voltier. Considering the, uh, friendly tone of the message, you would have to agree that any harassment on my part would have had to have happened after that date. Do you all agree?"

Every head bobbed in agreement. After all, it was the only thing that made any sense.

"Well, sirs, the only problem is such harassment would had to have taken place while I was in New Zealand with Ms. Cannes. Which I do believe would have been rather difficult considering we had no access to a computer. If you check the network files you will find there was no electronic communication between Ms. Voltier and myself during that time."

"Okay, Mr. Caruth. Point taken. Now back to this Sony business. When Ms. Cannes spoke to Ms. Voltier and the accountant, what did they say?"

Sydni answered the question without hesitation. "They assured me it was simply a lag in the accounting."

"However," Drew jumped back in. "Ms. Cannes was right. We invoiced the customer. The customer paid the invoices. But it wasn't charged against the purchase order. The invoices billed against the purchase orders was off by almost half a million dollars."

"What!?" The board room erupted into utter chaos. Sydni kept her seat and Drew kept his cool. Finally, Mr. Epps signaled for quiet, but the tempers in the room remained at a simmer. "Continue, Mr. Caruth."

"Turns out the money was being deposited and credited against another customer's account. There's only one problem."

"And what is that Mr. Caruth?"

"Said customer does not exist. Basically someone siphoned the money away. And since both Sony and the fictitious customer project were handled by the same person, it only makes sense that they would have a problem with me and Ms. Cannes sniffing around."

"So are you saying you were set up, son?" another of the senior partners snarled.

"I am, sir. It's all here." Drew tossed copies of his findings to each person sitting at the table.

"And was Ms. Cannes aware of your findings, Mr. Caruth?"

"No sir. She's finding out the same way you are, right here, right now."

Sydni sweated bullets. No wonder Drew wouldn't tell her what the hell had been going on. He wanted her free and clear no matter what happened. He could also say, truthfully, that he'd independently found the truth so no one could accuse Sydni of trying to take down another employee just to save her lover.

"And how did you come by this data?"

"I made my own copies and worked on them. Before I was suspended of course."

Each person present, including Sydni, looked through Drew's evidence. No one could deny its authenticity because it all carried the Expedex digital signature on every page. Finally, Mr. Epps and several others slammed the folders closed on the table and glowered.

Drew cleared his throat and said, "That's not all."

"You've got to be fucking kidding me." The senior partner cleared his throat, the blood vessels under his parchment thin skin flooding with color. "Excuse me."

"Thief or not, Alex couldn't have set up those customer accounts. Only someone with EVP or accounting roles on our network could do that."

"Who was it?"

"An employee named Alfred Pawn in accounting. But I think he was just being used by Alex. He didn't necessarily know what she intended to do with those accounts. All she had to do was deliver a signed requisition to the accountant and he would open the account no questions asked."

"So…"

"Only an EVP can sign one of those," Sydni burst out, unable to keep her cool for one second longer.

"Who was it?" Epps questioned.

"Jenkins, sir."

"Jenkins? As in, twenty year service award for outstanding direction, Jenkins?"

"Yes, sir. But I don't believe he's involved in

the plot," Drew assured. "Because Alex got Jenkins to sign the requisition when he was out sick. She claimed that it absolutely had to go through and that his being out that day couldn't hold up the process. So, Jenkins signed a blank form and faxed it to his secretary with instructions to give it to Alex. Of course he trusted her to complete it correctly. What he didn't know was that form would be used to create an account at First National, as we usually do, but when legal had the bank pull the files for the account, someone named Viktor Talent was listed as the Trustee instead of Expedex."

"Luckily for Jenkins, his secretary called both the accountant and Alex to confirm once she received the faxed form here at the office with nothing but Jenkins' signature on it. Then she smartly made notes in the files. Those files are time stamped and the calls are on the network's electronic call log with full records of when and to whom the calls were made."

"Shit!"

A quiet knock sounded, and Alex poked her head in. She immediately spotted Drew. Her eyes went wide for a second before a frozen façade slipped into place as she sat down in the nearest chair.

"You sent for me, Mr. Chairman?" she asked, all innocence and lace.

"Yes, Ms. Voltier. We understand you are the project manager for the Japanese accounts, namely Sony?"

"Yes, sir. Is there a problem?"

Sydni wanted to smack the bitch. She'd basically set Drew up with that harassment bullshit to get him out of her hair so she could complete her scheme. But what Alex hadn't counted on was the fact that her man was brilliant. And Mizz Voltier was toast. Burnt. No butter.

Syndi glanced down at her wrist and felt her cheeks flush with anger. It was almost time. Drew would face his accuser any moment now. She wondered what that bitch, Alex, would come up with to get out of this mess now that Drew had pretty much set up the pins for a knock down.

Another board member spoke up, as ancient looking as Mr. Epps, but with blazing blue ice-fire in his eyes and steel in his spine. "There is indeed a problem. But let's take care of what we originally came here for. Ms. Voltier we do not believe your claim of sexual harassment against Mr. Caruth has any grounds. However, we're not sure about the rest of it."

"The rest, sir?" Alex asked, still attempting to pass off her ruse of sweet-as-candy-ness.

Mr. Epps cut across her and addressed Drew instead. "You've presented a pretty solid case so far, Mr. Caruth. Is there any other proof, other than these documents, that Ms. Voltier is involved in espionage?"

"Espionage?" Alex snorted. Geesh, the broad just couldn't suppress the smirk that leaked out of the side of her lips to save her life. And Drew pounced. Sydni wanted to get up on top of the table and root him on.

Drew pinned Alex with a glacial gray stare, then turned toward the door and called out. "Please come in, Alfred."

The tall conference room doors eased open and Alex's pawn walked in.

Chapter Fourteen

Six weeks later

"Well," Charli said to her sister, "I think this is the most I've seen you enjoy life in, hell, I don't know how long."

"Try forever, Charli," Sydni grinned. After all, it was true, and it was all Drew's fault. The man attracted excitement wherever he went. Take all the drama at work with Alex and the espionage case. Sydni may have found the initial discrepancy in the documents, but in the end, it was all Drew. That first trip to New Zealand. Drew. Getting fucked like an animal up against a wall in a car port just off the beach? Drew. Enjoying life more in the past months than she had in years? Again, Drew. The man was insatiable, incorrigible…and damn stubborn. And Sydni couldn't have loved him more.

Sydni's stomach felt as if it had fallen down into her toes when the intercom beeped.

"I've got to run, Charli. We'll see you on Sunday?"

"Yep. Looking forward to it."

Flipping her cell closed, she tapped the intercom button and tried not to giggle. "This is Sydni."

"Mr. Caruth is here to see you ma'am."

"Thank you, Tsubaki-san. Send him in, please."

Seconds later, one of the double doors opened and Drew's beautifully dark head poked through. The man flashed a smile so devastating Sydni was glad to be sitting down because he simply made her weak in the knees.

"God, you are so damn fine," she blurted then blushed.

"Glad you think so. A man needs to hear that every now and then."

"You're so full of it. Every now and then, eh? How about every time we get together I'm forever telling you how gorgeous you are. Built like a tank, body like a god…"

"With a wicked cock to boot?"

Okay, now she was just getting plain hot. After all, the man was stalking her now with slow deliberate steps after he snicked the deadbolt to lock the door.

"While we're on the subject of hotness, Syd, you are the most beautiful woman I've ever known, inside and out."

Aww shucks. What could she say to that? Sure he'd called her beautiful, but it still tripped her heart to hear it. And to see the expression on his handsome face when he said the words. Sigh.

"And I have something for you, baby."

Then Drew was in front of her on his knees, pushing hers apart. Sydni felt her thighs heat in a flash. Oh yes, they'd covered this territory before. And her body knew exactly what to do—start creaming in anticipation of the lithe tongue headed its way.

Then...nothing. The man just sat there, looking into her eyes. His demeanor was just a bit strange. And he wasn't diving for her pussy as expected.

"Drew? What's wrong?"

"Nothing, Syd. Nothing at all. In fact, things couldn't be better." Easing closer he planted a sweet kiss on the inside of her left knee. "In fact...I need to ask you something."

But he still hadn't moved. Now she was really getting nervous. Sydni tilted her head and started to ask what was wrong again. Instead her mouth snapped shut with an audible click as Drew produced the most beautiful princess cut diamond engagement ring she'd ever seen.

"Oh my god!" Sydni gasped as her hand

flew to her throat. "B-but it's only been a few months. Oh my god. Oh my god!"

"A few months, sure. But I've waited a lifetime for you Sydni. Marry me?"

And that was the end of her composure.

So now she could add one more item to Drew's list of accomplishments — tears. Very happy ones. There was definitely no doubt. This man was better than Charli's homemade caramel kisses.

CONTINUE READING
to enjoy a sneak peek at chapters from
Wind and Fire, Gathering of the Storms
Book One, Volume I
by T.J. Michaels

Wind and Fire
Gathering of the Storms Book One
Volume One

by

T.J. Michaels

Chapter One

"Grandfather, if you must summon me from my pleasant dreams you could at least fashion a place more interesting," RuArk said softly into the darkness.

The room was stark, dimly lit, and completely empty — no windows, no doors. RuArk leaned against a rough wall with one foot propped up behind him, arms crossed over his chest. He smiled at the image of his favorite relative — an Elder known to all their clan as the Grandfather.

RuArk's brow furrowed as he watched the ethereal essence of the Grandfather's body shift and shimmer. Strange. It was as if he had difficulty staying with RuArk in a place where all was typically at the Elder's command. The Dream was a place where one was not confined to the body; able to move through time and space with¬out the inhibition of flesh and bone. There was nothing to fear, though things appeared vividly real. It was one of several places to seek wisdom and direction, or face your greatest challenges. As he gazed at the roiling image, he noted the deep frown marring the old man's ancient features.

When he finally spoke, the Grandfather's urgency-laced words formed as ice in the pit of RuArk's stomach. Gifts lost to all, except the Gaian, since the Breaking of the world gave protection to the wielder. Those without were vulnerable in this place. If they lost their way, their physical body remained in a state of deep sleep until they either managed to escape or someone guided them out. Unseen forces ruled this realm, and not all were friendly.

"The High Counsel of Draema sought us out in the Dream. Alone."

"Why would he do such a thing? He knows the risks better than anyone."

"He searched for your father to ask for your help," said the Grandfather. "Thank gods it was I who found him as he wandered."

"But why didn't he just come to me directly? I departed the High City not more than three days past. Negotiations were completed, and I am on my way home."

"Not any longer. You must return. This danger is focused on his daughter."

The coldness in RuArk's gut transformed into a 'berg, though it should be no surprise to learn 'that' particular female—Rhia

Greysomne—was in trouble. He hadn't seen her while he'd been in the High City this time. In fact, he hadn't seen her on any of his journeys to Draema Proper over the years. Though he hadn't sought her out, surely he would have heard of any threat to her?

RuArk tensed and pushed away from the wall. "Focused on Rhia? By who?"

"The High Counsel believes one of his own is responsible. He is wise enough to accept that he needs someone outside of his own province. Now, I have told you all I can. You will have to find the rest of your answers in the *Seeking*, and quickly."

The urgent energy that rolled off the Elder's image spiked.

"What aren't you telling me, Elder?"

The Grandfather usually epitomized calm…but not today. His anger-infused growl was cut off with a thick, veil-like silence as he took an uncharacteristic moment to gather himself. Not good.

Finally, he ground out, "There is a taint, a strange darkness in the otherrealms. When the Realmwalkers first noticed, it was quite subtle. Now it seems to have found a focus. It grows bolder, and nearer to the High Counsel's daughter. If you are not in the appointed place at the appointed time, the bringer of this taint will prevail."

"Prevail over what, Grandfather? Over who?"

"I cannot say. It is no longer safe here, even for our kind. But know that I have faith in you, akicita. As such, your Gift of Vision will not fail you."

RuArk's head tilted a hard left.

What Gift of Vision?

The ability to enter the Dream or go on a *Seeking* quest didn't count as a Gift considering any Gaian could do it. But the Gift of Vision? That was something different. In fact, RuArk had never manifested such a Gift. Or any Gift for that matter. While some of his kin had been late bloomers in this regard, RuArk's bud had been on the tree so long, surely it had dried up and fallen off by now. He opened his mouth to ask.

With a warm smile and twinkling dark eyes that crinkled in the corners, the shifting misty presence of The Grandfather shattered before snapping whole once again.

"Go. I will get word to the High Counsel to expect your return to the High City. I will guard over Rhia as best I can until then."

The Elder's shimmering image lost the battle of holding its form and winked out just as RuArk was tossed headlong out of the Dream and slammed back into his own body.

* * * * *

Rama Collaidh sat in his official offices. His fingertips itched to roam over the smooth desktop, to trace the rare veins of gray and silver threaded throughout the polished, white stone. At well past midnight, the window coverings were locked down tight. The dimmed iozene lamp over his workspace gave off the only light in the room. He liked the darkness. It offered a sense of comfort, sitting there surrounded by shadows.

Carefully laid plans were flipped back and forth in his mind — turned sideways and upside down in his mind as he examined them for any holes. Many of his fellow Council members considered him an ambitious, middle-aged nuisance. He could care less what his peers thought. He was in the prime of his life; wily and determined enough to achieve the impossible. And he had the High Counsel's ear.

Yes, his board was set and the pieces were

finally moving. Just as he noted a possible strategic problem, gooseflesh plumped just under the surface of his skin from scalp to fingertips. Sweat beaded between his shoulder blades before slipping coldly down his spine. In spite of the urge to shudder, Collaidh forced his stylus to move smoothly over the viewer embedded in the top of his desk.

He didn't bother to turn towards the source of his discomfort. There was only one person, one thing, that could make him break out in a cold sweat. Could enter his offices unseen. How long had the creature been standing there watching? Collaidh quickly dismissed the concern. His determination to have what he wanted was stronger than fear or foe.

"So, you've finally come," Collaidh muttered.

The words hung in the gloom for what seemed like eons.

"You summoned me, did you not?" The tone was flat, uncaring, and alarmingly similar to his own.

"Have you succeeded in reaching Rhia Greysomne?" Collaidh asked coldly.

Now the deep, silky voice took on a harsh edge of impatience. "Someone is protecting her now, warding her while she sleeps. I cannot summon her into the Dream at all. Yet before the warding began…"

"Get to the point, Behn. And step out where I can see you, damn it."

Collaidh forced himself to look directly into the white eyes of the thing's too-pale face. The only true color on the creature was its clothing. Even the thick, billowing tresses of his shoulder-length hair were white as full moonlight. Everything about him was unnatural. Yet for all that, how did he manage to be so bloody handsome?

Once he was fully into what little light there was, Behn smiled.

The grin chilled the blood. Collaidh's lip curled at the sight of gleaming, elongated incisors — longer than any normal man's. And slightly yellowed.

Must be from endless cycles of feeding.

The thought turned his stomach.

Yes, Behn spoke with sophisticated diction, but he was far from civilized. And only a fool would forget it.

"When asleep," Behn said, "a person without the Gifts is vulnerable once inside the Dream. Strangely, Rhia does not have this vulnerability. The most I could do was deliver the most fantastic nightmares. I believe I was slowly wearing her down, though I could not directly manipulate her."

"So what. Get to the point."

"We have encountered a problem. I am unable to touch her dreams at all now. She is either Gifted, or someone with the Gifts is protecting her."

"That's impossible!" Collaidh shot to his feet. Palm slammed against the sturdy desk hard enough to sting. "Her father is the High Counsel. The man is Draeman, through and through."

"What of her mother? Rhia is half-Gaian, is she not? Perhaps the mother has passed on a Gift?" Behn insisted calmly.

Collaidh frowned. Hell. He hadn't thought of that. Hadn't anticipated any of these delays. But he had to keep the upper hand. Behn had proven to be keenly intelligent, single-minded and ruthlessly ambitious—a creature that would take advantage of any perceived weakness. No one could know he'd enlisted the aid of a creature that shouldn't exist—one that had rediscovered how to manipulate magick long lost…

But then, who would believe it? After all,

this was Draema Province. Science ruled all.

With a smile that felt venomous even to himself, Collaidh pushed the thoughts away, deciding to force his point with his unwelcome, but much needed visitor.

"Look, the only people with Gifts are Gaian. Rhia's mother was, and remains, the only Gaian woman to marry outside her province since who knows how long. The woman is long dead, and certainly not around to teach her daughter anything about Gaia, Gifts, or anything else. And we all know the High Counsel hasn't tried in the least to teach Rhia anything about her mother's people since the girl was eight years old. Perhaps you're simply not capable of getting the job done?"

"Careful, old man."

Behn's feral growl sent Collaidh's heart into a stutter, but he was unwilling to give any ground. Collaidh ground his back teeth. This was his show to run, damn it. No way would he allow Behn to take control. He painted his face with a calm façade and refused to look away from the gleaming, white eyes. Eyes that seemed to bore right through his forehead.

"I said forget the High Counsel. We need that woman. We need Rhia, period." Settling back again into the plush cushions of his chair, Collaidh turned and unlocked a small drawer. "Perhaps this will help," he said as he held out a small amber vial filled with a milky looking fluid.

Collaidh steeled himself as perfectly manicured, long, semi-translucent fingers reached toward him. Little blue veins made various patterns underneath the smooth white skin. It made Collaidh's skin crawl when the lukewarm fingers touched his palm to retrieve the vial.

"What is this?" Behn asked.

"Don't worry about what it is. I called in a favor from a friend in the Society of Physicians. It won't harm her. Since the Dream business is no longer an option, you'll need to be more direct. This will make Rhia more cooperative."

"Fine. I will deliver it to someone who can get close to her. It must be done discretely if we are to avoid suspicion."

"I agree. You can't be seen here," Collaidh sniffed.

"If there is one thing I am good at, it is concealing myself from friends and enemies alike. And if I choose to be seen, I will simply be mistaken for my brother, would I not?

The sneer in Behn's voice was unmistakable. Collaidh grimaced at the bitterness in those words. Was it justified? Definitely. But he couldn't afford to be moved by it. Not now. Not ever.

"Perhaps," Collaidh responded, but didn't think it possible that Behn would ever be mistaken for his brother — a man who looked fully human, while it was obvious that Behn was...not. "But don't take any chances. I don't want anyone to become aware of your presence here. Besides, those teeth and eyes of yours would give you away for sure. You'd be shot on sight. What good would you be to me then? Unfortunately we need each other so let's make the best of it, shall we?"

"You promised to give Rhia to me. You will keep your promise, old man."

"Yes, yes, yes," Collaidh said, waving his hand dismissively. "I said you could have her once she's served my purpose. Now leave me alone. I have work to do."

Collaidh turned his back and ignored the wave of anger emanating from behind him. He didn't hear Behn leave, but was vastly relieved when the little hairs on the back of his neck finally stopped dancing.

* * * * *

Sara rose and donned a warm fluffy robe. She crossed the dark room to turn up the delicate-looking iozene sconces mounted on the walls. As she reached out her hand to adjust the brightness, her skin went cold. She was no longer alone. He was here. She expected no greeting and received none. He didn't care for niceties, only obedience.

"You will put this in the First Heir's teapot this morning. Do you understand?"

"I understand." Sara replied softly, her head tilted down in a genuinely terrified posture. "But her companion brings her breakfast in the mornings. How am I supposed to do this?" she asked on a shaky whisper.

"You will find a way, Sara."

She nodded quickly as he gave instruction and pressed a small glass vial into the center of her sweaty palm.

"Do you want to know what it is, sweet Sara?"

"N-No, sir. No, I don't." Sara clutched the vial firmly against her breast. Knowing too much simply wasn't a good thing with this man.

He moved closer, his long, dark coat swished against her bare ankles as he shifted behind her. His breath was both warm and cool against the nape of her neck. Darkness radiated from him.

She shivered uncontrollably.

"Good girl, Sara. Very good indeed," he crooned against her skin as his fingers skimmed lightly over her shoulders. Her mind said she should run screaming from this creature, but her body wanted him—wanted to feel the thick mass of snow-white hair slide over her skin. To feel his teeth scrape against her shoulder as he took her roughly. Her sex warmed and softened in need of the thick erection pressed against her backside. Ashamed, Sara closed her eyes against her physical reaction to such an unnatural man. When she opened them again, she was in bed.

Blinking into the darkness, a wave of relief swept over her. It was a dream. It always seemed so real. Even the sensitive buds of her nipples puckered at the false memory of his breath wafting over her skin. She rose, wrapped her robe closely about her body, and went through the motions she could have sworn she'd already done. Slipping her hands into the warm pockets, Sara went dead still when her fingers wrapped around a small glass vial.

"How in blazes does he do that?" She almost wished she had the courage to ask him. Almost.

She washed up quickly. Dressed in her Houseman's uniform, she slipped the vial into her trouser pocket. As she rushed to the kitchens, Sara pushed away guilt for what she was about to do. Failure equaled pain — lots and lots of brilliantly delivered pain — courtesy of a much too-handsome devil that was supposed to exist only in dreams. Unfortunately for her, he didn't seem inclined to stay there.

Chapter Two

By the time Rhia made it to the dining hall, she looked and felt like every description of hell she'd ever read about in the old story books. In addition to the sweat and dirt stains that covered her tunic, her leggings sported a long, jagged rip. The fabric flapped annoyingly as she walked, baring a good amount of thigh. She'd almost had her leg sliced open in the middle of teaching the final knife-fighting session of the day. Good thing she hadn't been instructing laser whips instead. Geesh.

She pushed the thoughts away, and instead focused on what awaited her upstairs in her rooms — a blasted bath, and she couldn't wait to sink into the warm…ewww!

She sniffed and then sniffed again. Was that rank smell her, or the filleted protein on her plate? Not wanting to offend, Rhia ate quickly at a table closest to the wide double doors and headed up to her apartments.

The twitchy burn in her legs made her hiss out loud as she climbed the tower stairs. Wiped out, and absolutely tired of being so damn tired, she forced herself to trudge on. Why did her place have to be on the only floor that couldn't be accessed by a lift?

Finally at the top of the tower stairs, she reached for the key around her neck. Her hand brushed the sharp corner of a note she'd completely forgotten about. Removing the crumpled piece of paper from her breast pocket, Rhia immediately recognized her father's bold, flowing script. Even bolder words had her bristling before she was halfway through the short missive.

To: Rhia Greysomne, First Heir to the Seven Colonies of Draema Province

Consider this a formal reprimand from the Office of the High Counsel. I don't have time to run all over the City looking for you as you take on more and more responsibilities. I had to send a Houseman to find you to deliver this note. I'm sure he's just catching up with you and it's probably well past dinner time as you're reading it.

"Damn it, how does he always know?" she wondered aloud.

You are hereby relieved of all duties except for the diplomatic responsibilities of the First Heir. In addition, you may teach one, and only one, combat or blade class. All of your other duties related to the Society of War have been assigned to other officers. Further, you are to leave at first light for Harbor Station to inspect the two new airships built for the coastal patrols. You will also inspect the troops stationed there under your brother's command. Joan Rouillard and Brita Shae will accompany you. To make the journey shorter, I've assigned you a hover driver. He'll take you to the train, where you'll board for Harbor Station. And no, you may not take the outmoded form of transportation you prefer — that damned horse of yours.

It was bad enough he was making her take the train to the harbors, but she wouldn't be allowed to even transport herself to the station? Not that she knew how to operate one of the hover things anyway, but that wasn't the point. And Moonlight was not outmoded, damn it!

With an annoyed huff, she finished reading.

I advise you to find time to enjoy yourself while you are at Harbor Station, young lady. You will come to my offices before you leave to pick up a message for your brother. When you return to the High City, your life will change considerably.

Regards,

Grey Greysomne, High Counsel of Draema

Province

Commander in Chief, Society of War

Her father had sent a note to tell her off. This was a new experience. Grey Greysomne usually delivered any displeasure directly to her face. But a note? Geez, how impersonal could you get? And what did he mean her life would 'change considerably' when she returned from Harbor Station? And why did she need to go inspect a ship or troops?

Her younger brother was the Harbormaster for a reason. That man knew all there was to know about the blasted vessels. What a total waste of time. But as one of the highest-ranking officers of the Society of War, she had her orders and would obey them. Of course she wouldn't admit to being secretly pleased with the opportunity to visit her brother and his family. Perhaps she'd rest better there.

Rhia cringed as she recalled the weeks of nightmares so terrifying, so wrong, that she'd jerked herself awake with a scream on her lips. There'd been several nights where she'd awoken with sweat-soaked bed linens stuck to her body as she sat huddled in the center of the bed. She was sure her skin had tried to crawl away and hide a time or two.

But last night everything had changed. Sleep had been peaceful and strangely calm with the presence of an old man. Her dream had been simple — the man seemed to enjoy nothing more than keeping her company, and the nasties had stayed away. It would be nice to drift off and not wonder what was in store. Maybe some rest and a change of scenery would do just that. Perhaps Harbor Station was the ticket.

Rhia read the note again, stuffed it back into her pocket, and fumbled with her key tag. The flat, square fob gleamed dully in the bluish light of the iozene lamps set into the walls. Holding the tag to the center of the panel next to the door, a familiar click indicated the release of the lock.

One step into her private domain, Rhia felt the cares of the day melt away. This space was uniquely hers. It was strategically unsound to have walls an enemy could hide behind, so there were none in this space. Instead, it was large, airy, and tastefully arranged so she could see from one end of the suite to the other without obstruction.

The sleeping area was dominated by a huge, curtained bed, but it was the floor that defined the space. It was covered with soft, gray, hand-knotted carpets. Where the carpets ended, so did her sleeping area. A large mosaic of tiny gray and white tiles in the shape of the sigil of the House of Greysomne covered the dining area floor. It was centered by a large table; its base of polished marble was topped with a thick, smoky glass pane. Off to the left was the mantel covered with awards and weapons, over a wide, and thankfully blazing, iozene fireplace.

A few steps past her large, four-post bed, a chilly wind sent the silky bed curtains billowing. The mid-winter breeze flowed through the glass doors that led to her private balcony… Only she was sure those doors were closed and locked this morning. Brita would have been the last person out of these rooms, and she would never have left them unsecured.

Shivering from the whoosh of cool air, Rhia dropped her blade and belt down on top of the dining table with a loud clunk as she passed. She pressed the little switches that controlled the wall of thick, beveled panes and waited impatiently as the glass slid silently along the tracks.

The moment the balcony doors closed, her trouble meter tipped off the scale. Turning ever so slowly, she peered into the darkness. Sharp senses tried to see and hear everything at once as her eyes adjusted.

The open curtains let in the glow of a half-moon, whose light was obscured by a passing cloud. Looking past the mantle, Rhia peered toward the bathroom entrance. The sheer curtains that gave her privacy were pulled open as usual.

However, what was unusual was the shadowed figure standing there. A black cloak swirled around a body as it took a step forward, and the "it" was revealed as a man.

"Hello, Rhia."

Bryan Collaidh? Aw hell. She hadn't seen him since she'd made First Blade, cycles ago. The haunted look on his face, and the dark shadows under his eyes, made it obvious those cycles had not been kind. His pale skin stood out in stark contrast against lackluster, shoulder-length black hair. Didn't he know greasy hair was out of style in Draema? And what was with the all-black garb?

The creep hadn't left the province under the best of circumstances. As far as she was concerned, he was still unwelcome in the High City, and certainly unwelcome in her personal space.

"What the hell are you doing here?" she

asked, not bothering to hide the contempt in her voice.

The lines of his mouth hinted at the cruelty she knew he was capable of. A malevolent black gaze followed her steps. Deep set, and round as old-fashioned playing stones, his eyes seemed too large for his face. He looked like an overgrown guppy, complete with thin, pouting lips. An image popped into her head of this unwanted guest, complete with gills and fins. His lips glub-glub-glubbed as bubbles floated up towards the surface of the river she wanted to drown him in.

Her amusement faded quickly as she considered the situation. It took a bold man to break into her apartments with no fear. Why would he take such a risk? The answer was obvious — he still didn't have any goddamn common sense.

Rhia watched him closely as she walked across the room. The glowing fireplace halfway between them cast his smooth, black clothing with an eerie, orange tint.

"I asked what you're doing here, Bryan." At the mantle now, she stretched her hands toward the warming flames, appearing completely at ease.

"I've come to visit you, old friend," he drawled, moving slowly toward her. He attempted to smile, but it must have made his face hurt. The skin appeared to freeze just around his mouth in the middle of the feeble attempt.

"Old friend? What are you, nuts? I haven't seen you since the day you decided to use my face as a punching bag."

"I'm a changed man, Rhia. Cycles of surviving on the borders can do that to a person." He ground out the words as his gaze seemed to focus on something far, far away. Some called the borders "Hell's Eastern Seventh Level." Judging from the menace rolling off of her nemesis, like dust clouds of choking malintent, the name must be pretty accurate.

She took a deep breath, then another. Blast it, she'd always been calm when meeting a foe. But she'd never faced a known enemy whose very presence dragged one of the worst moments of her life out of the locked dungeon of her mind.

But her typical pre-fight calm was nowhere to be found. No, she was torqued the hell off. And this wasn't going to end nicely.

She almost smiled.

Biding her time, Rhia leaned against the smooth mantle with one arm draped casually atop the ledge. Her fingertips brushed the hilt of the specially commissioned blade her father had given her on her sixteenth birthday. For a few seconds she considered pulling the razor sharp work of art down off the mounting, but changed her mind. The blade was too special to dirty on the likes of Bryan Collaidh. Too bad she didn't have a laser pistol handy. At least those left wounds that didn't bleed much. Rhia was sharp enough to know that this little conversation was going to end in a fight, and the less blood on her tile, the better. She hated cleaning blood out of crystal grout.

Then she noticed that Bryan wasn't moving. Simply stood there, wasting her time.

"Look Bryan, I'm tired. I had a long day, and I really don't feel like being bothered. I was so busy this evening I was two hours late to dinner. Now I'm two hours late for bed. Can't you just go away? Perhaps we can talk in the morning." Knowing she didn't mean a word of that last part. After all, there was nothing to say.

"You have grown into a beautiful woman, Rhia. And I think I'd rather talk now. Besides, I've returned to Draema Proper for one purpose.

To claim you."

Laughter bubbled up out of her throat before she could stop it. She just couldn't help it. Claim her? Ridiculous! Her smile was genuine, but her thoughts took another turn, and her insides turned with it. What if he was serious? A serious lunatic, that is. He wanted her? Why? He certainly didn't love her. She didn't think he even liked her.

Sigh.

Okay, he had about an inch on her in height, and maybe twenty pounds in weight. The calculations only took a moment. She could take him down fast, then call in a favor to a couple of the soldiers who roomed on the floors below. The advantage of living in her father's Citadel – it only took seconds to get someone up here to help drag the body away.

But Bryan still hadn't moved. Not even to blink. Perhaps a reminder that she outranked him would push him over the edge so they could get this over with.

She rolled her eyes and said sleepily, "Get out, you idiot. Otherwise, as the highest ranking officer in the Society of War, I'll personally have you assigned to the iozene mines with all the other miscreants."

Then she waited for him to lose it like he had long ago, when he'd taken a closed fist to her face. Her offense—a rank promotion ahead of him. Angry and full of jealousy, he used his failure as an excuse to abuse her. In his mind, the anger had been all her fault. Personal responsibility? Puh. Those two words weren't in his vocabulary.

Hands raised in surrender, he headed toward the door. Halfway there, he changed direction.

Damn it.

He looked back and forth, between her and the katana lying on the table. The metal under the black leather, which crisscrossed elegantly over the handle, gleamed dully in the moonlight. Bryan picked it up, testing the weight of it in his hand.

Calculation flared in those cold, black eyes as he took a single step, pivoted and threw the weapon clear across the room. It bounced off a wall near the front door with a loud clang. She had no doubts now—the man was definitely nuts.

From rage to cool civility in a blink, he crooned, "I hear you've made Blademaster well before the usual ten cycles. But it doesn't matter whether you're a Blademaster or not, we're going to reinstate our former engagement."

Bullshit.

One hand on her hip, she took an angry step forward. "My father didn't approve of you back then, and he certainly won't approve now. Besides, if you were on the up-and-up, you wouldn't have broken in and waited for me in the dark. What the hell do you really want?"

"Give me a minute. I'm sure you'll figure it out." He lunged.

* * * * *

Rhia was ready, and ducked past him so fast he found himself facing the fireplace with nothing but air where she had been seconds before. A clean kick to his kidneys from behind slammed him chest-first into the mantle. The wind whooshed from his lungs. After a few wheezing breaths, he faced her with eyes drawn tight in an angry frown. And a bit of…shock?

"Surprise, asshole."

He hadn't expected her to be able to defend herself without a weapon. Well good. But she'd rather have a blade between them. Rhia ran for her steel.

Bryan dove, taking her feet out from under her. She went down hard, skinning her cheek on the smooth, hard mosaic under the dining table. But stinging cheeks were a relief. If she'd landed a few more inches to the left, her jaw would have made solid contact with the glass and marble of the table.

She rolled over with a groan and was happy to be in absolute pain rather than knocked out cold.

Then he was on her, trying to capture her hands as they connected with his eyes, cheeks, and lips. Rage, thick and palpable filled the bit of air between them.

"I'll have what I want whether you agree or not, Rhia." Pant. "Once I fuck you." Snarl. "I'll present evidence to the Council."

What the hell?

"Your honor," he sneered as if she had none, "will require you to declare me your mate. Our houses will be joined one way or another. Good thing you were altered at the Age of Consent. Without a hymen, at least it won't hurt. Much."

Whoa. How did he know when she'd been altered? And what the hell else did he know? The records of every member of the Society of War, especially hers as First Heir, were classified. No one knew her secret other than her father, and her friends, Brita and Joan.

Her mind screeched to a halt. The law was clear. As female First Heir, she'd had her hymen painlessly removed at the Age of Consent as required. But afterward, Rhia didn't have the Draeman privilege of screwing around.

While mates, lovers and Sensuan were carefully recorded for all members of the Society of War, for Rhia the rules were a bit different. She had two choices—she could take an assigned lover for a time, whose identity and time of service were carefully determined and recorded.

Or she could take a mate. Period.

Her mate's identity would remain secret for a time until she declared the union to the Council, or proof of consummation was given. Vows could be taken in the presence of her father and a witness, or she could elope. This was to keep the First Heir's mate from being assassinated before he could actually say, "I do."

No one, especially Bryan Collaidh, should know that her records were clean – no assigned lover, no mate. If he managed to prove he'd had sex with her, she was screwed. And not in a good way. No recourse. No way out.

Except to get free. Right now.

Rhia jerked her hand loose. A fist connected with the side of Bryan's head, sending it sideways with a wicked snap. The jeweled dagger always strapped to her thigh was almost in her hand when the bastard dropped his full weight down on top of her. She just couldn't get a full breath. Her head spun. Wriggling black spots swam around her field of vision.

Ugh, she was going to throw up.

A backhand to the jaw didn't help. She hadn't seen the blow coming and now both her hands were above her head, held securely in his grip. His free hand brutally squeezed and twisted a tender breast. And he had an erection? Ewww.

She swallowed hard as more bile surged and her dinner bubbled threateningly at the base of her throat. Frustrated and angry, Rhia let out an ear-piercing scream when Bryan pushed his hand roughly underneath her tunic searching for the top of her leggings.

When the skin of a clammy hand touched the flesh of her belly, she went completely still.

"That's more like it, bitch," Bryan growled, yanking on her already ripped and torn clothing to expose her underwear. "I knew you would see things my way, Rhia. You always were a mewling little puke. It's your fault I ended up on the borders all those cycles. Your fault! If you hadn't run to your father blaming me for your making me angry, I would have surpassed your rank by now. You deserved a beating then, and you deserve one now."

Wasn't there an old proverb in the ancient books that said pride goes before destruction? Obviously the man wasn't much of a history reader.

In his haste to dip into her goodies, he released her hands to get a better grip on her bottoms. Her elbow crashed into the middle of his throat. Suddenly he was the one having trouble breathing.

Now wasn't that just too bad?

Knee to the groin preceded a full-contact left hook. He rolled completely away, eyes watering as he gasped through his bruised windpipe. It seemed he couldn't decide whether to hold his throat and gag, hold his balls and moan, or soothe his swelling eye.

On her feet, she yanked up her leggings and retrieved her blade from the carpet near the door. The corner of her mouth lifted at the exact moment Bryan realized the only way out was through her securely locked balcony windows or the front door. The first option was a no go. But a four story fall wasn't high enough to knock any sense into his hard head anyway. And unfortunately, Rhia and her blade stood in front of option number two.

There was a third option—part him from the family jewels he'd tried to force on her moments ago.

"You wouldn't kill a man in cold blood. You don't have it in you." But the quaver in his voice said he didn't believe his own words. He knew she'd do it. Knew she'd shred him. Sweat dripped from his brow and trailed down his clammy pale skin like wax down a spent candle.

Neither of them heard the door open.

Chapter Three

His party had shown none of their discomfort or concern in their expressions at the suddenly pressing journey back to Draema Proper. In fact, if not for the chilling mounds of snow piled along the roads and the biting winds, it would have been a good time under clear, and amazingly vivid, blue skies.

They'd moved quickly through the buffer zone that separated Draema Seine from the capital of the province, Draema Proper. In the distance, the High City had been a welcome sight, rising from the heart of these lands. Built in the middle of its seven colonies, this was the most advanced area in the world. The dawning sunlight had reflected various shades of pink and purple off both the inner, and outer walls; all of which were built with the famous, silvery-white Draeman stone.

Sleek buildings were shaded by tree-lined walks, which led into vast, city squares. The High City boasted a mix of rolling hills, and neatly-groomed pastures alongside well-kept roads. Some were laid with cobblestone, while others were covered by a smooth, dark, magnetized substance that allowed the passage of small conveyances called 'hovers'. Horses were still used here for sport, but inner-to-outer city travel typically meant a ride in one of the neat little vehicles, or a spot on the train. RuArk preferred the wild, open spaces of his own province, but didn't hesitate to admit this place held wonder for those who appreciated such things.

He'd brought more than thirty men on this journey, but only RuArk and a single fireteam of six warriors had passed through the open City gates this morning. There were very few of his people in this place, yet he'd been immediately recognized.

The advantage of being son of the ruler of the neighboring province was being waved through the towering gates quickly. Well, that, and the reputation of being a ruthless bastard that took down enemies hard and fast with no promise to ask questions later.

Through a second set of lower walls that surrounded the Citadel, the High Council's right-hand, Mannon, had greeted them and rushed them into a meeting. From this morning's arrival, until leaving the High Counsel's chambers moments ago, they'd worked through one planning session after another until everything was in place.

Though so tired his muscles weighed down his bones as he dragged himself toward the guest apartments, RuArk could not ignore the flash and tensing of excitement that tapped at his gut. As if something long dead was waking inside him, stretching and unfurling itself in anticipation of seeing where this new turn in life would lead.

And Rhia was smack in the middle of this, this...whatever it was.

And in spite of the intrigue surrounding the danger to the woman, what would occur between them would be hot as the mid-Summer sun. He'd known from the *Seeking*, had felt it as he'd replayed that vision over and over in his mind. Damn near ached for it now that he knew the woman was somewhere near. Strange, he still hadn't seen the flesh and blood star of his *Seeking* vision. But he would soon enough.

RuArk steered his First Commander, Sharyn, toward a wide archway that opened into a large, starlit atrium. The space was filled with lush green trees, shrubs and a little stone bench where one could sit and enjoy the sun or moon overhead. At the rear of the atrium, two sets of mirroring staircases took off up the tower walls to a landing; where tall arches led opened to wide hallways. The stairs continued up the walls, winding their way upward to another landing, and yet another.

Finally they were at the top. There were no hallways or arches — only two doors separated by a ten-meter wide, colorful mural of the Draeman countryside.

He'd just pressed the key against the wall lock of the rooms he would share with Sharyn when a panic-inducing yell rang through the tower. He looked toward the sound and cursed.

Sharyn's gasp of surprise, followed by her quiet chuckle made him grimace. He hadn't meant to say that out loud, especially in the presence of a lady. The High Counsel put him in this part of the Citadel to keep an eye on Rhia. He'd hoped the job could wait until she returned from the made-up errand they'd created for her at Harbor Station.

"Apparently not," RuArk muttered and moved quickly towards the source of the noise. Through her slightly open door, two voices were clearly heard, both of them yelling. Not wanting to be mistaken for an intruder, he opened the door carefully, just enough to peek inside. The scene that met him was…wrong. On too many levels to list.

A greasy looking fellow had Rhia flat on her back on the thick carpets, trying to rip her trousers off. She was obviously not cooperating. The man's fist connected with her jaw. The blow should have knocked her out, but Rhia was moving and moving quickly. Her next breath saw her up off the floor and brandishing a wicked, long blade. A katana made in the old style.

Her intent was clear — skin the greaser.

Rhia's hair was dark, fire streaked and tangled all over her head. But the blood. There was so much blood. It was on her face, streaming down her neck from her eyes, nose and mouth to soak the collar of her top.

RuArk kept his expression neutral, but he really wanted nothing more than to rip the greaser in half. Hell, he might not love Rhia yet, but it was only a matter of time considering the Ancestors clearly meant for him to have her. The moment he'd accepted the *Seeking* she'd been given into his care. And this man dared to threaten her? Not bloody likely.

His first thought was to kick the door in the rest of the way, stride across the room and grab the idiot by his scrawny neck. But he'd be a fool to simply stroll into the room and surprise a woman with a sharp blade in her hands and hellfire in her eyes.

In spite of the obvious injuries, her fighting form was perfect; her handling of the blade smooth and experienced. She held no fear and knew she was in position to deliver a killing blow. And he couldn't blame her one bit. In truth, it was Rhia's ability to handle her visitor that helped keep RuArk's anger in check.

RuArk anticipated her move, knew the exact moment she'd decided to slice open the greaser's chest. What was she thinking? The scandal it would cause — a man in her rooms this time of night, and a dead man at that. Not to mention all the blood and guts that would have to be cleaned up.

And it would ruin his investigation.

One step through the door, RuArk called out.

"Excuse me. Is there a problem here?"

* * * * *

Rhia glanced away from the groveling swine on the floor and looked into a pair of eyes of such a wondrous mix of gray and silver, they reminded her of the waters off of Draema's southern coast.

RuArk Miwatani—the bane of her childhood existence. A bane she hadn't seen in so long she was surprised she recognized him. It was the eyes. Stormy sea, silver-as-fog, captivating eyes. Simply unforgettable. Ever. She had to look up a bit to meet his gaze, but once she caught it, Rhia was stuck right there.

Blazes, he was simply breath-stopping. Gone were the boyish good looks and mischievous expression. In their place was an angular jaw, high cheekbones and the confidence of a man.

A long, thick, black-as-sin braid was pulled forward over his shoulder to brush against the middle of his stomach. His skin, though quite a bit fairer than her own, was such a warm bronze that even now, at the end of mid-winter, he appeared to have spent a good deal of time under the glorious sunshine. He wore an unadorned, dark gray, fine gauged tunic, with dyed-to-match trousers. The outline of thick, roped muscle was visible beneath the supple material.

He closed in on her with a step so light she still didn't hear his footballs even though she was looking right at him.

And how the hell was she noticing this in the middle of a life or death struggle?

And what the hell was he doing here?

As far as she was concerned he was yet another man in her space without her damn permission. Enough gawking. Back to business.

Rhia returned her attention to the weasel groaning on the floor and raised her katana for the final blow. But before she could take a step, RuArk grabbed Bryan by the collar of his finely appointed cloak, and the back of his finely appointed trousers, hauled him out the door, and tossed him down the closest staircase.

While Bryan tumbled, Rhia's attention remained on RuArk. Sure, his expression was firm but she could tell he was totally enjoying this.

She looked him dead in the eye — or tried to, given his typical tree-like Gaian height — and proceeded to tear his head off with her tongue.

"Look, asshole. I know you warrior types are used to throwing the muscle around, but this is Draema. Here, people don't interfere unless they're asked to interfere. If I'd needed help I would have…"

Mouth snapped shut. The most beautiful

woman she'd ever seen stood directly behind the most ruggedly handsome man she'd ever known. Humph.

Bone straight, thick, and black-as-midnight hair was partially covered with a length of translucent silk that could only be described as sensual. Actually, her entire outfit seemed to be one big wispy scarf. Her skin reminded Rhia of the summer fruits that, according to the histories, used to grow in the now non-existent southern locales so long ago.

"Peaches," Rhia whispered, though she truly hadn't meant to.

And if this female had stood here the whole time, then she'd seen Rhia act a complete fool.

"Blasted hell," she muttered.

Rhia knew her hair was a tangled mess. Her face was swelling and surely beginning to display various colors in addition to sweat and blood. She wasn't sure why she cared that this man might compare her raggedy, torn appearance to this exotic woman. Nope, she shouldn't give a bloody goddamn…but she did. In fact, she flew past 'caring' and skidded to a halt at 'mortified'.

She scowled. Maybe the blows Bryan had landed on her face had shaken her brain loose because there was no way she should notice how ridiculously delicious RuArk's lips looked with that bit of a smile spread over them. Gah.

"What do you want? Aren't you far from home?" she snapped, forcing a blizzard into her words.

"You screamed. Loudly," he said quietly as he stepped toward her slowly, carefully. His words may have been just as frosty as hers, but the look he gave was equal parts 'smoking hot' and 'royally pissed'. "I can't resist taking care of such a beautiful lady, especially if she's in distress."

RuArk's voice slid over Rhia's frazzled nerves like warm, honey syrup while his expression took on a mysterious quality; like he could see through her funky-assed mood straight into her head, to uncover all the secret thoughts swirling around in there. Thoughts of him.

"Anything else I can do to assist you?" he asked quietly, though no less firm and as bossy as ever. And he was entirely too close now and looking at her as if he knew something she didn't. Her ice began to melt. Fast. She shivered, but not from fear nor an adrenaline crash.

It was anticipation? But of what? And who?

Not RuArk, for sure.

After all, she'd known this man forever. Though he'd been a boneheaded, spoiled, king's son, she'd carried a torch for this particular pain-in-the-ass for years. Memories she'd pushed to the very fringe of her mind peeked its head up and over the ragged edge of her conscience.

She remembered RuArk, putting straw in her hair. RuArk besting her at wooden blade practice. RuArk pulling stupid pranks on her, and getting her in trouble with both their fathers.

Sigh.

RuArk holding her hand at her mother's funeral, wiping the tears from her cheeks and telling her it would be okay. RuArk wrapping her in his cloak while she huddled in misery as they left the burial grounds so far away in Gaia province.

RuArk singing to her — quite badly at the top of his lungs — on her tenth birthday after talking his father into bringing him on an unscheduled visit, just to give her a birthday present he'd made with his own hands.

RuArk telling her he was going away to train for his role as Protector of the Realm of Gaia.

RuArk, staying away for years.

But it didn't matter now. Since then, Rhia had made a couple of trips to her own personal hell and back. She'd become her own woman—a woman who would never need saving by anyone. Ever.

And that included the gorgeous man towering over her.

"You should visit the Physicians, Rhia. It's getting late. I will escort you, if you wish."

So he was trying to save her, and tell her what to do? Not. Her out-of-whack-ness dissolved, replaced by a wash of hot anger. And a bit of unexplainable fear. Rather than dealing with the latter, she squashed her emotions into the toes of her blood-spattered boots and straightened her already-ramrod spine.

"Fuck. Off. RuArk."

She nudged him out the door with the tip of her katana, and practically punched a hole in the wall lock panel. The door slammed shut. So what if her behavior was irrational. Who cared? Besides, nobody asked the big guy to appear out of nowhere? To toss that pig, Bryan, down the stairs when she would have rather given him a few choice cuts?

Did it matter she'd been a shrew to a man

who'd always set her pulse racing and put her senses on edge? Or that she'd bled all over the place in front of an exotic looking woman in a daringly sexy outfit, all after learning via a stupid note that she'd been stripped of everything that made her who she was?

Rhia stomped around her apartments hurling every curse word she'd ever heard her soldiers use, then switched over to a couple of different languages just to draw it out a bit longer. She soon found that growling and cursing weren't enough. She yelled her frustration to the top of her lungs.

* * * * *

"She was so grateful for your help. Really, I could tell just as she slammed the door in your face."

RuArk turned to scold a not-so-amused Sharyn, but snapped his mouth shut at Rhia's cursing, loud enough to hear through the thick door. Sharyn scowled but didn't say another word, choosing instead to disappear into their suite across the landing and head to her own bedroom.

As for RuArk, it had been a long time since

he'd had a reason to see humor in anything but a good fight, yet here he was smiling, then laughing outright. The sound rumbled up through his chest in a deep, full timbre. And all because of the fate the Ancestors handed him, a fate named Rhia.

Door secured, he slipped his blades underneath his pillow and burrowed down into the thick, downy bedding. Keen senses detected no danger as he relaxed and closed his eyes to meditate.

The rest of his men had slipped quietly into the City and settled into the non-descript, seldom used quest quarters on the far side of town. At dawn, Rhia would depart for Harbor Station on the errand they'd made up for her, and RuArk would visit the High Counsel to finalize the details of their plans.

After her behavior tonight, he almost wished the High Counsel was going to be the one breaking the news to the hellcat next door. Almost.

He and Rhia's first meeting after so many seasons had been far from expected. He'd expected happiness, and light, and fun...then again, he had enjoyed tossing the greasy fellow down the steps. In the end, it didn't matter whether Rhia liked that he was here for her or not, he had a job to do—keep her safe and make her his.

As he drifted off, the *Seeking* quest he'd taken after his visit from the Grandfather flashed to the forefront of his mind…

Carried on the arms of the Wind, RuArk looked down upon the land with admiration. The beautiful, rolling hills were covered by a spectacular white, snowy blanket that sparkled like diamonds and luminescent pearls. The bright, full moon reflected off the frozen meadows. And there were so many stars. They filled the pre-dawn sky, twinkling their greeting to the Wind as It passed, carrying its companion.

Off in the distance RuArk spotted a faint glimmer on the ground. The light appeared to be a small campfire, out in the middle of the ice-covered lands. What would anyone be doing way out here in mid-winter? They circled around as RuArk searched for any signs of life. The place was deserted.

"What's going on here?" RuArk asked on a whisper.

The Wind gave no answer, but instead settled directly over the small flames, whipping them up into a firestorm. It flared wildly in spite of the snow covering the ground. The energy from the fire joined itself to that of the Wind, and the Wind became a great storm also. Side by side, the firestorm and the windstorm grew together, reaching up into the starlit sky until it seemed brightened by a second sun.

Then RuArk felt it, just as the Grandfather said. A taint. A subtle hint of foul aura just out of reach, focused on the flame. It faltered until it ceased to give as much energy to its union with the Wind. As the flame wavered, the windstorm and the firestorm were both diminished. The mighty forces of nature became nothing more than a slight breeze and a small campfire once more.

Here, just as in the Dream, he didn't experience true physical sensation, but only a fool would ignore the trickle of apprehension slipping up his arms. He turned to the North, but saw nothing. South, East and West, all was silent. But he knew something, someone, was out there. Perhaps multiple some ones.

After endless moments, he spotted a woman alone in the night, gliding along the snow-covered meadows. The sleek outline of her body was shrouded in shadow. She moved with easy grace. Careful yet confident, she possessed an inner strength that made her appear more hunter than prey. Who was this woman, now almost as near as his own skin?

Looking more closely, RuArk almost tumbled out of the Seeking and back into his physical body in surprise. The glow from her amber eyes pierced his soul – Rhia Greysomne, daughter of the High Counsel of Draema Province.

Oh, he remembered Rhia, stubborn and headstrong as a young girl. He was now being set on the path back to her as a woman. There was danger, yes, but he sensed that she needed something more than protection. But what could she need more than her own life?

It had been endless seasons since he'd seen her, yet even after all this time, and in this place, his body reacted strongly to her presence. Gods, her essence was exquisite; her aura strong and clean. She was not the source of the foulness on the air. But whoever, or whatever it was, seemed to follow her, long for her, covet her from a distance. Strange.

RuArk reached out but she didn't respond. Didn't seem to sense him at all.

Flashes of himself and Rhia in a loving embrace danced before his eyes. They smiled, touched, arms twined around each other as he loved her fiercely. Then there were stolen moments, a few quiet words shared.

My gods, she was his? A woman he'd thought of often, but hadn't pursued? Had longed for, but believed was out of reach? RuArk had no idea how things would develop, but it wasn't his to worry about. All he needed to do was find and stay on the path that had obviously been chosen for him. A path that led to Rhia Greysomne.

After accepting what had been shown to him that

night, he'd been returned to his physical body. And there he'd sat until gooseflesh had risen on his bare arms and legs. In fact, he'd watched the sunrise through the opening of the Seeking place and breathed in the lingering scent of sweet, warm female until it had completely faded away.

And now, the woman of his *Seeking* was just across the landing. Just out of reach. RuArk rolled over in his bed and let the memory of the *Seeking* continue to wash over him and fill his mind even as sleep claimed him. She was his, and he would protect her from whatever danger lurked here in Draema.

And RuArk couldn't wait to begin his new job.

About the Author

TJ is a USA Today and New York Times bestselling author, as well as an award-winner in several romance genres, including paranormal, fantasy, sci-fi and urban fantasy romance. A true Taurus, TJ isn't slowing down and she's definitely too stubborn to stop when she sees the fence!

No matter the genre TJ is penning, her favorite thing to do is build worlds. To take you somewhere extraordinary. To transport you to a place where you can close your eyes and slip into your fantasy…

Visit T.J. Michaels online at her website www.TJMichaels.com

Also by Author TJ Michaels

Carinian's Seeker, Vampire Council of Ethics Book
One
Serati's Flame, Vampire Council of Ethics Book Two
Hatsept Heat, Vampire Council of Ethics Book Three
Seeker's Solace, Vampire Council of Ethics Book Four
Silk Road, Seals of Destiny
Spirit of the Pride, A Pryde Ranch Shifter Story
Niah's Pride, A Pryde Ranch Shifter Story
Pursuit of Pride and Pleasure, A Pryde Ranch Shifter
Story
Juicy, A Twilight Teahouse Story
Luscious, A Twilight Teahouse Story
Jaguar's Rule
Forever December
Egyptian Voyage
On the Prowl
Entwined Hearts
Elemental Heat
Caramel Kisses